D1492059

SILVER RIVER RANCH

When Blount Roberts challenged Val Dixon to a duel with short knives, he chose the weapon with which he was convinced he could kill Val. But Val, who had been tutored in the art of steel by an old Karankawa Indian, survived to tell the tale, and won himself an implacable enemy in the person of the man he had got the better of. He also incurred the wrath of Blount's twin brothers and his father, and of all of the Roberts clan except the daughter, Rosalee. But Rosalee's sympathy also had a barb. For she was apparently in love with Craig Sherwood, a man even more dangerous then her own menfolk to Val's security.

SILVER RIVER RANCH

Leslie Scott

First published in Great Britain 1963
by Wright & Brown, Ltd

This hardback edition 1997
by Chivers Press
by arrangement with
Golden West Literary Agency

ISBN 0 7451 4712 7

*The characters in this book are purely imaginary and bear no
relation to any living person.*

British Library Cataloguing in Publication Data available

Printed and bound in Great Britain by
Redwood Books, Trowbridge, Wiltshire

SILVER RIVER RANCH

CHAPTER ONE

THE TWO MEN fought silently, save for the hissing pant of their laboured breathing. Blood streamed down their faces, spurting from their wrists. Their naked torsos were dyed crimson. Dark gouts splotched the grey dust of the street.

The knives flashed in the sun, clashed with a dull tinny sound as strokes were parried awkwardly, for the left hands of the duellists were securely tied together with rawhide. Scarlet drops were flung from the points of the three-inch blades. The shortness of the blades prohibited the likelihood of a single fatal stroke, so the fight was a gruesome, gory slashing match as the contestants hacked away furiously. No quarter was asked or expected.

One man was tall, lean, broad-shouldered, with black hair and grey eyes. His bloody lips writhed back to show white, even teeth. His opponent was shorter, more massively built. His hair was a bristly red, his eyes so dark blue as to seem black; they glowed hotly as he struck and parried. He was a few years older, being somewhere in the early thirties.

A ring of spectators leaned forward eagerly as the strokes went home and the blood spurted.

"They can't keep it up much longer," one muttered. "They're both bleeding like stuck pigs. Anybody who gets mixed up in a Helena duel is a plain fool."

The movements of the battlers were growing slower, the blows losing force, for both were weakening from loss of blood. But their red-streaked faces were grim, their jaws hard set. With failing strength they stabbed and slashed.

The end came suddenly. The burly man sagged and reeled back as far as the restricting thongs would permit. His taller adversary drove his knife home, the blade sliding squarely between two of the other's ribs, the haft guard thudding against the flesh.

The recipient of what might well prove a lethal wound fell, dragging the other down on top of him. The blood-drenched pair lay motionless in the dust of the street.

"All right," said an authoritative voice, "cut them loose and pack them over to Doc's place and see what he can do for them."

The white-bearded old frontier practitioner snorted with disgust as he viewed the ripped and gashed bodies.

"A pretty mess!" he growled. "Darn loco young coots! Well, young blood is hot and can only be cooled by letting it flow now and then. Lay 'em on the tables and I'll patch 'em up."

First he drew the knife from between the bulky man's ribs. He studied the injury for a few moments, then nodded his grizzled head.

"Not a wind wound," he said. "Didn't catch the lung and missed the arteries. Doesn't 'pear to be any internal bleeding. A couple of inches higher, though and he'd have been a goner."

Working swiftly and expertly, he stitched the various cuts, applied a few bandages and, as soon as they regained consciousness, gave each man a strong sedative.

Then he put them to bed, in separate rooms of the rambling structure he called his hospital.

"Now the rest of you hellions behave yourselves for a day or two," he told those who had packed the injured men from in front of the Silver Rail Saloon across the way. "I ain't got space for many more, so try and stay in one piece till I clear this place out."

Although he had suffered the only really dangerous wound, Blount Roberts, the bulky man, was first out of the hospital. Out of the hospital, in his saddle, and out of sight. Doc Beard insisted that Val Dixon remain in bed for another day or so.

"He got you one good one in the left wrist; nicked an artery," the doctor explained. "You bled plenty. Val, what was this all about?"

"I braced him about something and he challenged me," Dixon replied shortly.

"He's got a reputation for being a first-class knife man," Beard commented.

"A deserved reputation," Dixon conceded.

"Well, you'll have a couple of scars on your face to remember him by," said the doctor. "Not too bad, though. Didn't get you much there."

"He fought mostly for the body, trying to shove that short blade under my ribs," Dixon answered.

"It's a wonder he didn't do it," growled Doc. "If he had, it wouldn't have been the first time; he's poison with a knife. No slouch with a gun, either, but cold steel's his favourite. Well, I'll amble out and corral you something to eat. Yes, you can get up tomorrow. Stay in bed the rest of today, though. Be seeing you."

After the doctor left the room, Val Dixon lay thinking over the events of the past few days, and not particularly enjoying the review. In truth, he was just a little ashamed of the business. Viewed in retrospect, it appeared so senselessly melodramatic.

Not that he'd had much choice in the matter after Roberts had reacted to his show-down. Roberts didn't "reach," as Dixon had fully expected he would. Roberts didn't know how good Dixon might be with a gun or how fast on the draw, but a man who packed two guns in holsters slung low on the thighs would always bear watching. So Roberts chose what he thought would be the safer way. Roberts had intended to kill him when he'd challenged him to the Helena duel, knowing that Dixon could not refuse the challenge if he wanted to hold up his head in Star Drive Valley. There was no doubt in Dixon's mind as to Roberts' intention. And Roberts, with a well-earned reputation of being a peerless knife fighter, had been confident that he could kill his enemy with little more than possible superficial injury to himself. The vicious upper stroke under the left ribs, if properly executed, could prove fatal even with the short-bladed knife the Helena duel demanded. And Blount Roberts was a master of that stroke.

What Roberts didn't know was that Val Dixon had been taught knife fighting by an old Karankawa Indian he had befriended, and the Karankawas were the top knife fighters of all the Texas tribes. Dixon could have killed Blount Roberts when the latter, weakened by loss of blood, sagged away from him. It was not by chance that his blade had entered Roberts' body at a spot that would not necessarily prove fatal. Val Dixon wasn't a killer yet.

While he lay thinking, Dixon was under discussion in the Silver Rail Saloon across the street.

"Yes, Dixon came out on top, as nobody figured he would. But just the same, I wouldn't want to be in Val Dixon's boots," said John Cooley, the owner. "The Roberts family has run Star Drive Valley and the rest of the section for years, and they don't take kindly to a stranger coming in and refusing to knuckle under to them. And now he's downed the big he-wolf of the pack, they'll really be after him. Dixon is in for trouble."

"Uh-huh, but looks like Dixon is a cold proposition himself, giving Blount Roberts the lie to his teeth that way. And I figure he don't wear those two guns for ornaments," remarked a young cowboy.

"Right," agreed Cooley. "But you had an example, too, of how tricky the Robertses are. Blount sets up to be a top knife fighter, and he is. So he didn't reach, as everybody thought he would. He just grinned that grin of his and challenged Dixon to a Helena duel. Dixon couldn't back down, and Roberts knew it. He figured to kill Dixon easy, like he has a few others who braced him. Made just one mistake, one he didn't figure on. Seems Dixon is a top knife fighter, also. And Dixon made a mistake, too. He didn't kill Blount Roberts when he could have easy enough. A couple of inches higher with that drive between the ribs and it would have been curtains for Roberts."

"Maybe he slipped," hazarded somebody.

"Nope, he didn't slip," said Cooley. "I was watching close. The blade landed right where he wanted it to. He wasn't out to kill Roberts unless he had to save his own life. And there he made the mistake."

"Reckon he just ain't a killer," remarked the cowboy.

"He ain't, but the Robertses are liable to make him one, if he manages to stay alive long enough," said

Cooley. "And look out for a peaceful jigger who don't really hanker for trouble. A stick of dynamite is all right if you let it alone, but don't put a match to the fuse. That's the way with those quiet fellers. Whack 'em too hard and you get an explosion that's liable to blow you to smithereens."

"How'd all this ruckus start, anyhow?" asked the cowhand, who was new to the section.

"Well, I guess it started when old Salmon Walsh took a notion to die," Cooley replied. "Salmon Walsh was one of the real old-timers here; his family settled in Star Drive Valley not long after the Roberts did, and that was a lot of years back. His spread, the Cross W, was at the south-west end of the valley, south of Silver River, which really ain't a river at all; just a big creek. The Robertses' big Walking R takes in nearly the whole north-west of the valley and runs way up in this direction. Couple of ranches between here and the Cross W, on the south side of the river, and one on the north side, before you get to the Walking R.

"Well, Salmon Walsh followed through with his notion and did die. He was a bachelor and his only kin was a sister over east at Galveston, who didn't take no stock in the cow business; she's a schoolteacher and pretty close to Salmon's age, I reckon. Now the Robertses had had an eye on the Cross W for quite a spell. They aimed to buy it when Salmon passed on. It would round out their holdings nicely, giving them control of the whole west end of the valley."

"Why didn't they?" asked the cowboy.

Cooley chuckled. "That's where Val Dixon came into the picture," he said. "Seems Dixon went to school under Samanthy Walsh, and it 'pears she was sort of fond of him and figured him to be a up-and-coming youngster. He was working as range boss on a spread north of Galveston and used to visit the old lady when he came to town. So when Samanthy told him that Salmon had passed on and that she figured to sell the holding, Dixon told her he'd like to buy it. Seems he'd saved up enough pesos, along with some he inherited from his father, to make a reasonable down payment and figured the ranch could pay off the rest in time. That suited Samanthy, who I guess has always been eating regularly and not hankering for much money. She called it a bargain and signed over the Cross W to Dixon."

"So Dixon sort of beat the Robertses to the draw," observed the cowboy.

"Uh-huh, just about," said Cooley. "So when the Robertses got in touch with Samanthy and made her an offer, she told them no dice, that she'd already sold. They made the mistake of offering a bigger price if she'd go back on her bargain with Dixon. From what I heard, the old gal got considerable riled and in nice ladylike language told them that she didn't deal in the double-cross and had a darn poor opinion of folks who did. That's what she told Blount Roberts, who'd been sent over to handle the deal; told him to his face. Didn't set over well with Blount, I reckon, but there wasn't anything much he could do about it. So I guess he decided to take it out on Dixon. Anyhow, when Dixon showed up and took possession, old man Clanton Roberts, the *padre* of the clan, rode to the Cross W and proceeded to tell Dixon what he was to do and wasn't to do in Star River Valley. Clanton being an old man, Dixon wasn't over rough with him, but I understand he told Clanton, polite like, to mind his own business and that he wasn't taking orders from anybody as to how he would run his holding. And the feud was on.

"So you see Dixon and his less than a dozen riders are up against Blount Roberts and his two brothers, Crane and Wilbur, and the old man Clanton, who ain't no push-over, and their near thirty hands."

"And don't forget the gal," added Anse Potter, who owned the P Lazy A. "Rosalee can sling a gun with the best of 'em."

"That's right," agreed Cooley.

"But why did Dixon jump Roberts in here like he did?" the cowboy asked.

"Blount had been sounding off around town, saying that they were losing cows and that he figured they went south-west to Mexico," Cooley explained. "Dixon heard about it, and when he met Blount in here, he told him he was a liar. You saw what happened next."

The cowboy nodded. "Dixon's men sticking with him?" he asked.

"Reckon they are," said Cooley. "A couple of them were in to see him yesterday. He brought his outfit with him from over east. Salty-looking bunch, too, but nobody hereabouts would work for him and buck the Robertses."

The cowboy suddenly grinned, with a flash of crooked but very white teeth, a funny twisted grin that moved only one side of his mouth. There was a twinkle in his pale, cold eyes. He was boyish-looking, slightly under medium height, and slender.

"Dixon hiring?" he asked.

"Reckon he would be if he could find anybody to hire," said Cooley. "I've a notion he's short-handed.

His holding ain't over small and sort of hard to work. Why?"

"I could use a job riding about now," the other replied.

Cooley stared at him. "Son," he said, "you're a fool."

"Reckon I am," the cowboy conceded cheerfully, and headed for the door.

"Where are you going, son?" Cooley called.

"To see Mr. Dixon," the other replied over his shoulder as he passed through the swinging doors.

"Well, I'll be darned!" remarked Cooley. "Who is *he*?"

"I don't know," said old Anse Potter, "but he somehow reminds me of a young feller I once saw over in New Mexico, quite a few years back."

"Who?"

"Feller named Bill Bonney—Billy the Kid," replied Potter.

A sudden silence fell as Potter pronounced the name of the dreaded outlaw who, although only twenty-one when Ranger Pat Garrett killed him, had watched more than a score of hard men go down under his flaming guns.

"Well, I'll be darned!" Cooley repeated. "Tom, you're right. He does remind you of Billy the Kid."

"His name's Billy," said Cooley's head bartender. "Billy Flint. Leastwise that's what he said it was when he was talking with me the day Dixon and Roberts had the fight. Left right after and didn't show up again till today. Yep, Billy Flint. 'Pears to have plenty of money to spend. Notice he packs two guns, too."

Tom Potter tugged his moustache. "I've a notion," he said thoughtfully, "that if he does sign up with Dixon, that pair will give the Robertses something to think about."

CHAPTER TWO

VAL DIXON LOOKED up in surprise as the young cowboy entered the room. Billy Flint came forward and introduced himself.

"Understand you could use another hand or two, Mr. Dixon," he said.

"I could if I could get them," Dixon admitted.

"Well," said Flint, "Here's one you can get. I've been riding the chuck line and don't like it."

Dixon studied him a moment. He liked the boy's looks, although there was something about his pale, watchful eyes that gave him a slightly disquieting feeling.

"You'll quite likely be signing up with trouble if you ride for me," he warned.

"I heard all about it, and watched you give Roberts his come-uppance," Flint replied, adding, "And I've signed up with trouble before. I'll take a chance."

"All right," Dixon said, "you're on the payroll as of today. Need money to sleep and eat on till I get out of here?"

"Nope, much obliged," Flint answered. "I got a room over the stalls at the livery stable. Like to sleep close to my horse."

Again Dixon experienced a certain sense of disquietude, but he only said:

"Okay, I hope to leave here sometime tomorrow.

We'll ride to the spread together. I gave a couple of my hands orders to be here day after tomorrow, but I believe I can make it a day earlier. Feeling better than I expect. Don't figure to have any trouble on the ride."

Billy Flint grinned again, that queer, white-toothed, twisted grin.

"You won't have any trouble," he said evenly. "I'll be ready when you are, Mr. Dixon."

With a nod he left the room, seeming to glide rather than walk. Dixon gazed after him, turned his head and remarked to a crack in the ceiling:

"Now what have I tied onto? 'Pears to be all right, but that grin of his reminds me of a wolf raising its lip over its fangs."

After giving Dixon a careful once-over the next morning, Doc Beard decided it would be safe for him to ride.

"But take it easy," he cautioned. "You don't want to be bustin' those slices open, especially the one in your wrist. They're not fully healed yet, and you've had about all the blood-lettin' that's good for you for a while. Somebody riding with you?"

"Yes, I think so," Dixon replied. "A young fellow I hired yesterday. Name's Flint. I've a notion he'll be across the street at the Silver Rail."

"While you're eating your breakfast, I'll amble over there and see if he's around," said Doc. "I'd prefer for you not to ride alone. You could get into trouble, you know, if your cayuse happened to stumble or something."

Dixon had a notion that Doc Beard was thinking of something other than stumbling horses, but he merely nodded.

"Much obliged," he said. "Bring Flint over if you find him."

Dixon had not yet finished eating when Doc reappeared with Billy Flint in tow.

"I'll get the rigs on the broncs, Mr. Dixon," Flint instantly volunteered. "Yours is the big red sorrel, I believe the stablekeeper said."

"That's right, but be careful," Dixon warned. "Rojo doesn't take kind to having a stranger lay a hand on him."

Again the queer, lopsided grin. "I get along with horses—all horses," Flint said, and glided from the room.

Dixon was willing to agree when, a little later, he stood on the porch and watched Billy Flint appear with the horses. He was not leading them—the split reins were knotted together and looped over the pommels. He was walking between them, and each animal had a nose resting on his shoulder.

How the devil, Dixon wondered, did a chuck line-riding cowhand tie onto such a superb mount as the tall blue moros that paced sedately beside his own splendid sorrel?

Billy Flint paused in front of the porch. He glanced up the long main street that was a continuation of the broad trail flowing from the mouth of Star Drive Valley a mile to the west.

"Muerto," he remarked. "Funny name for a town. Means 'The Dead,' don't it?"

"That's right," Dixon replied as he descended the steps. "And it earned its name, back in the old days. Plenty woolly yet, but not what it was then. Well, guess we'd better get going. A twenty-five-mile ride ahead of us. It's a big crack in the hills, the valley, forty miles long and close to twenty wide. Sort of rough in places, too, but fine rangeland."

"It is," agreed Flint, as they mounted and started the horses moving. "I rode down it and back the other day."

"The devil you did!" said Dixon, shooting him a quick glance. "Why?"

"Oh, I heard folks talking about it the day you had the ruckus with Roberts, and thought I'd like to look it over," Flint explained. "I liked the looks of it and figured I wouldn't mind working there. So when the fellers in the saloon mentioned you could use some more hands, I braced you for a job."

"I see," said Dixon. "Then you'll have noticed, if you rode clear to the west end, that some of my holding won't be easy to work."

Billy Flint shrugged his lean shoulders. "I've worked worse," he said, "in Arizona and in Mexico. Some real tough going down there in Sinaloa, but I liked it and hated to leave."

"Why did you leave?" Dixon asked curiously.

"For my health," was the short reply.

Dixon noted that Flint, in addition to his black-handled Colts, carried a Winchester rifle in a saddle boot under his left thigh, Texas Ranger style. Flint's watchful eyes intercepted his glance.

"You ought to pack one, too, things being what they are hereabouts," he said. "Sixes against a long gun is sometimes lopsided odds."

"You're right," Dixon conceded soberly. "I will from now on."

For several miles the trail ran down the middle of the valley; then it forked, one branch veering rather sharply to the north, the other slanting south. Dixon followed the south branch.

"This is the old trail," he explained to his companion. "The one over there to the right was run after folks began settling in the valley."

A little later they splashed through the waters of a fairly broad stream that flowed from the south, curved gradually and continued its course in a westerly direction, gradually veering away from the trail.

"Silver River," Dixon said. "Comes from under a cliff over to the south and runs right down the middle of the valley till it passes my holdings—it's the boundary line between my land and the Robertses'—then turns south through a canyon and continues to join the Rio Grande. The trail parallels it through the canyon. It's a gloomy crack, and I was told that quite a few battles were fought in there between smuggler trains and robbers."

"Interesting section all round," Flint commented cheerfully. "Yes, I'm going to like it."

Star Drive Valley was not really a valley in the true sense of the word, but a series of sedimentary depressions bulwarked by mountains. To the north were the lofty ridges of Woods Hollow Mountains, with the jagged mass of the towering Glass Mountains rising beyond. To the south the Pera Blancas shouldered the sky and a ripple of lesser ranges rolled away to the mighty bulk of the Santiagos.

Hills started up from the floor of the depressions, sometimes in short chains, sometimes in single spires like tombstones of long-dead ages. But the level or rolling land was clothed with needle and wheat grass and curly mesquite that could fatten a steer's sides in no time.

"We're passing across Anse Potter's P Lazy A," Dixon remarked. "Next is Craig Sherwood's Forked S, a small spread, and then my holding, the Cross W. Over the other side of the river is Van Purdy's Lazy TV. After the Lazy TV the Roberts ranch begins and runs all the way to the west end of the valley."

"A big one," commented Flint.

"Yes, it is," agreed Dixon. "A good one, too, but I figure my land is a bit better, although it's not much more than half as big. I've got better water, and the canyons in the hills down there, while they're hard to work, are grass-grown and have springs and provide good shelter."

Hour after hour they rode, at a moderate pace, for Doc Beard had cautioned Dixon to take it easy.

Finally Dixon announced that they had reached Cross W range. All the way down the valley they had passed clumps of cattle. Now Flint eyed the cows coming into view with distinct approval.

"Good beef," he commented. "The best I've seen here yet."

"First class, all right," Dixon agreed. "Old Salmon Walsh, the former owner, had been going in for improved stock for quite a while. He was getting good results."

They had covered a few more miles when ahead a chain of hills started up from the level range. Soon they were skirting their base. "As I said before, that's why my holding is hard to work," observed Dixon, gesturing towards the rugged brush-grown slopes. "Those bumps are full of narrow canyons and gullies and dry washes. The cows hole up there, and combing them out is something of a chore."

Billy Flint nodded absently. He appeared to find the nearby slopes interesting, for his gaze kept roving over them, searching the tangle of thickets from base to crest. He spoke without turning his head.

"Someone up there pacing us."

Dixon gazed up the slope but, although his eyesight was much better than average, could see no sign of movement amid the brush.

"You sure?" he asked.

"Yes, I'm sure," Flint replied, still without turning his gaze from the slopes. "He's trying to keep out of sight, but I spotted him a while back. Watch that bit of open space ahead; he'll have to cross that. Likely to cross it fast."

Dixon fixed his eyes on the gash in the growth that had been scored out by a rock slide from the crest. Another moment and he saw a moving blob, dark against the grey of the denuded slope. It was fully six hundred yards distant from where they sat their horses, perhaps a bit more, but he was sure it was a horse and rider.

"Told you so," said Flint. "Now watch." His hands moved as he spoke. The big Winchester flipped from the saddle boot. Flint threw the long gun to his shoulder and fired in one flickering movement. Dixon saw a black speck sail through the air. It was the distant horseman's hat. The rider himself flashed across the open space and out of sight.

"You shouldn't have done that," Dixon protested. "The fellow may have just been riding around up there."

"On your land, isn't he?" Flint countered as he ejected the spent shell and replaced it with a fresh cartridge. "And anybody who paces you and tries to keep under cover ain't up to no good. I figured to give him a scare. Decided not to kill him. Maybe I made a mistake."

Val Dixon drew a deep breath. Billy Flint had meant what he had said.

Dixon took the initiative. He veered his horse sharply and swiftly to the right, and didn't resume the westerly course until he had but five hundred yards more between them and the spot where the hatless horseman had vanished.

"Gent might take a notion to return the favour, and we're in the open," he observed.

"Uh-huh, he—" Flint began, and ended with a crackle of oaths as something sang past over their heads. To their ears came the whiplash report of the distant rifle.

Still swearing, Flint threw the Winchester to his shoulder again and sprayed the growth with bullets.

"That should hold the hellion," he growled, reloading with smooth speed. "A hit at twelve hundred yards would be plain luck, but if we let him keep on trying the son might get lucky. I've a notion he heard my blue whistlers talking to him, though, and sifted sand. Didn't I say I was going to like this section!" His lip lifted in his twisted grin.

Dixon shook his head and they rode on, keeping a sharp watch on the slope, where Dixon could spot no signs of movement.

"Maybe you got him," he remarked. Billy Flint shook his head.

"Nope, he's still going," he replied. "Look over that manzanita thicket up there to the front."

Straining his eyes, Dixon could make out a dot bouncing about in the air above the growth.

"That's a bluejay," said Flint. "Shot up in the air a minute ago like a popgun ball. That means he's scared of something passing under his nest. It's that drygulcher heading for a place where he can get over the top of the sag without being spotted. Wonder what he *was* doing up there? Waiting till he could get a good shot at you, the chances are. I'd say somebody left town ahead of us when they found out you were going to ride today."

Silver River had veered slightly to the south, and now they were riding not far from its banks.

"Right about here is where I met a couple of fellers the other day," Flint announced. "Husky fellers, red-headed, like the jigger you had the fight with."

"Sounds like Crane and Wilbur Roberts," Dixon commented. "Did they have anything to say?"

"Asked me what my business was down this way," Flint replied. "I told them it wasn't none of theirs."

"What did they have to say to that?"

"Didn't seem to like it," Flint replied. "The biggest one—"

"That was Wilbur," Dixon interpolated.

"The biggest one," Flint repeated, "he sort of reached towards his belt. Stopped before he got there."

"Hm," commented Dixon. "From what I've heard, Wilbur Roberts usually finishes what he starts."

"Guess it was finished before he got started," said Flint. "I told them it would be a good notion to ride back the way they come, and to keep on riding until they were out of rifle range. They rode."

Dixon could read between the lines. Evidently Flint had got the drop on Roberts, and they had wisely obeyed his order. Otherwise it was quite likely that the Roberts family would have been two short.

"They'll have it in for you for that," he observed.

"Folks have had it in for me before now," Flint said. "And some of them ended up wishing they didn't," he added grimly.

Shortly afterwards they saw a big old ranch-house advantageously situated on the crest of a rise in a grove of ancient live oaks.

"There she is," Dixon said.

Billy Flint eyed the ranch-house and the other buildings with evident pleasure.

"Looks like a home," he commented.

"It is," Dixon said. "The boys like it. They came along with me from over Galveston way and seem plumb satisfied."

"Why not?" said Flint. "Good cow country, good man to work for, and nice neighbours." The grin flashed. "Yep, no doubt about it. I'm going to like it here, too."

The sun was touching the western crags and threw a mild and chastening light over the rangeland and the rugged mountains when they rode into the ranch-house yard. Nine or ten punchers streamed out of the bunk-house, waving hands and shouting greetings. A grizzled old waddy bowlegged forward to shake hands with Dixon.

"Bob, this is Billy Flint, who's signed up with us," Dixon introduced his companion. "Billy, meet Bob Turner, my range boss. He'll hand out the powders."

"How are you, Flint?" said Turner as they shook hands. "Glad to have you with us."

A hand offered to put up Flint's horse. Turner led him to the bunkhouse. Dixon, his own horse cared for by another hand, entered the living-room of the ranch-house and dropped wearily into a chair. He was weaker than he had thought.

CHAPTER THREE

WHEN DIXON AWOKE the following morning he was greatly improved. After a leisurely breakfast and a couple of cigarettes, he walked about the ranch-house grounds, looking over things in general, and finding everything functioning properly. The hands were all out on the range, checking and tallying for a shipping herd Dixon had resolved to start rolling soon.

It was a beautiful morning of blue skies and golden sunshine, and Dixon abruptly decided that it would be a good notion to take a ride. So he saddled Rojo, the big golden sorrel. Following Billy Flint's advice, he attached a saddle boot to the rig and thrust his heavy Winchester into it. Telling the cook he'd be back sometime in the afternoon, he set out at an easy pace, following the trail, which now veered slightly southwards.

After several hours of easy riding he approached the beetling end wall of the valley. Here the trail curved sharply to the south, paralleling Silver River. Not far off, trail and stream entered the narrow cleft of a canyon which was the route to the wild country leading to the Rio Grande and Mexico. About a mile east of the canyon mouth the trail branched. One fork, very narrow, little more than a game track, after running through thick and tall brush slithered crookedly up the slopes of the hills that formed the south wall of the valley, by way of which their crests could be reached.

The main branch of the trail, also flanked by growth, entered the canyon, following a bench often not more than ten feet wide, with the stream dashing and foaming against its rocky banks a few yards below. For Silver River, which down the valley had been broad and shallow and placid, was here a brawling torrent, deep and narrow, flecked with boiling rapids.

Dixon had never ridden all the way through the canyon. Today, with leisure time on his hands, he decided to see what the country beyond its south mouth looked like. He sent Rojo into the gloomy gorge. The rocky walls were almost sheer, and in some places the beetling cliffs overhung. There was evidence of rock falls during the time of the spring thaws, but there was not much danger of loosened fragments thundering down in the dry summer weather.

The sun was high in the sky now and its slanting rays struck the cliff far above his head, for the trail hugged the east wall of the canyon. Looking up, it was as if he gazed into a suspended sea of molten flame, the light refracting in shattered rays from the various mineral outcroppings. The opposite cliff was purple with shadow and was somewhat lower, its crest less jagged.

The canyon was a good five miles long, and it took him better than an hour to reach its terminus, which opened onto a plateau. The stream now ran at the bottom of its own miniature canyon until it reached a stratch of level land beyond, where it quickly widened.

From where Dixon sat his horse the view was splendid. Before him were the far-flung ramparts of the Big Bend wilderness. Mountains piled on mountains, their lofty crests kissing the sky and shouldering aside the clouds. The mightly range of the Santiagos marched south by east to become the Carmen Mountains of Mexico. Dixon was fascinated by the kaleidoscopic miracle spread before his eyes and could not tear his gaze away from it. He was something more than halfway through the canyon when his abstraction was jolted by a sound high above his head, a sharp crackling utterly alien to the breathless solitude.

It was his concentration on the colourful cliff across the way that saved him. He saw the vast shadow rushing down the striated wall and knew what it meant. He drove his spurs home and shouted to his horse.

Rojo leaped forward his own length and lit running. With a thundering crash that shook the mountains, a mighty mass of stone struck the trail at the very heels of the flying sorrel, peppering horse and man with stinging particles. It took a fifth of a mile of struggle to bring the frantic animal under control. Looking back, Dixon saw that for a stretch of fifty feet or more the trail was covered with huge fragments of rock.

A cold sweat broke out on his face. His hands trembled. Had he been but a few yards farther down the trail, horse and man would now be but mangled flesh and splintered bone.

He glanced up at the cliff crest, where a long ragged gash, gleaming whitely, showed where the fall had originated. He stared in bewilderment. How had such a split taken place in dry, still weather? It just didn't make sense unless—

He recalled the crackling explosion he had heard just before he saw the shadow rushing down the opposite canyon wall. It *could* have been caused by the loosening rock tearing way from the parent body, but it had ominously resembled a dynamite explosion.

CHAPTER FOUR

VAL HAD RIDDEN about a mile when from somewhere in front, and seemingly high in the air, came the sharp, hard note of a rifle shot, followed almost instantly by a fusillade of reports low down and somewhat farther ahead.

Dixon stiffened in his saddle and drew his Winchester from the boot.

However, there were no more shots. He rode on, watchful and alert. Abruptly he thrust the rifle muzzle to the front. Directly ahead the trail curved slightly, and from the far side of the bend came a drumroll of fast hoofs. He pulled up and waited, his eyes fixed on the bend.

Around the bulge of the cliff careened a single rider going at top speed. Dixon recognized the slight figure of Billy Flint. Flint raised his voice in a shout.

"You all right?" he called anxiously as he slowed his horse and drew rein beside Dixon. His face was bleak, his eyes like splinters of sapphire in his bronzed face. The left sleeve of his grey flannel shirt was smudged with a dark stain.

"Fine as frog hair," Dixon replied. "What's happened back there? What was all the shooting about? And how come you're down here?"

"We came back to the *casa* at noon for some chuck," Flint answered. "I was first in. The cook told me you'd ridden west, alone. I lit out after you."

"Why?" Dixon asked.

"Because I don't figure it's safe for you to be riding alone, that's why," Flint retorted. "I guess maybe you figure the same about now."

Dixon's reply was a nod.

"I had a hunch you'd be heading for this canyon," Flint resumed. "I was out on the prairie a couple of miles when I heard what sounded like a dynamite blast cut loose up in the hills. Didn't sound good to me, so I speeded up. Guess I got a mite careless, and came near paying big for it. I *was* sort of watching the hills, though, and I saw the glint of the fellow's rifle barrel when he pulled the trigger. Nicked me in the arm instead of drilling me dead centre. The smoke showed me where he was and I cut loose on him with a magazine full. He came rolling down through the brush and lodged against something about halfway up that snake track that goes up the slope. He's still there, all right. What happened in here?"

Dixon told him, in a few terse sentences. Flint didn't appear overly surprised.

"Figured it was something like that," he said. "I saw just about the same thing done once before; only the jigger they were after stayed under the fall. I ain't much of a praying man, Mr. Dixon, but right now I'm thanking the Good Lord that you didn't end up the same way."

"Amen," Dixon said fervently. "Let me look at that arm; then we'll go see what you bagged. I've got bandage and some salve in my saddle pouch; always carry them."

"Just a scratch," Flint deprecated his injury.

"Maybe," Dixon answered. "Then again maybe not;

you've been bleeding quite a bit. Light off and we'll have a look-see."

The wound proved to be an ugly gash in the fleshy part of the upper arm. Dixon smeared it with the ointment and applied a bandage.

"That should hold it till later," he said. "Bleeding has almost stopped. Try to favour it, though."

"Keep your long gun ready for business," Flint warned as they resumed their ride through the canyon. "There's just a chance another fangin' sidewinder might be hanging around."

They approached the canyon mouth warily, but there appeared to be nothing inimical around. Even more cautiously, they rode the brush-flanked trail until they reached a spot from which they could see the side trail winding up the slope. They studied the crooked track for some minutes before making a further move.

"Looks okay," said Flint. "Birds going about their business up there. Guess we can risk it." They put their horses to the track.

The drygulcher lay on his back, two bullets through his heart, his fixed eyes glaring up at the blue sky. He was a hard-looking specimen, his mouth a cruel, bloodless gash across his swarthy face. He was lean and lanky, showing evidence of Indian blood. His rifle lay nearby.

"The sort you can hire anywhere on the Border to do a killing for a few pesos," Billy Flint commented. "One of the Roberts bunch, do you know?"

"To the best of my knowledge, no," Dixon replied. "During the four months I've been here, I think I've seen all the Roberts hands at one time or another. Don't recall ever seeing this one before."

"I'd say they'd hardly use one of their regular riders

for a chore like this," Flint observed thoughtfully. "Let's find his horse; it should be around somewhere."

After a bit of searching they located the animal tethered to a tree, a good-looking cayuse. The rig was ordinary, with an empty saddle boot.

"Mexican skillet-of-snakes burn," said Flint, after inspecting the brand. "Don't mean a thing. What shall we do with the man?"

Dixon thought a moment. "We'll leave him where he is," he concluded. "I don't see there's anything to be gained by packing him to town and the sheriff. I gather the sheriff is an honest man, but I expect he is beholden to the Robertses to a certain extent. They might try to make something of it. Let whoever sent him come and find him."

"Doubtful if they will," said Flint. "That is, unless they get over curious as to what happened down here. Anyhow, there'd be no tying them up with that try to kill you. Evidently this snake was working alone."

"Guess you're right about that," Dixon conceded. "I'm no range detective and wouldn't know how to go about pinning it on the Robertses, even if I thought there was a chance to do so. We'll get the rig off the horse and head for home. I figure you did a mighty good chore," he added.

Flint's twisted grin flashed. "I don't like folks to throw lead at me," he said. "Made it sort of personal, as it were."

"Rather personal for me, too, after what happened in the canyon," Dixon said grimly.

They had covered a few miles when they saw a horseman riding down from the east at a leisurely pace. Flint stiffened and dropped a hand to his rifle butt.

"Now what?" he wondered in growling tones. It

struck Dixon that when Billy Flint was more than usually on the alert, his voice changed subtly, became harsh and deep.

Dixon studied the approaching horseman and recognized the tall blond man whose unusual good looks were slightly marred by marks of dissipation. "It's Craig Sherwood, who owns the Forked S to the east of my holding," he said. "He's all right."

Flint grunted, but did not relax.

Sherwood waved his hand and shouted a greeting. A few minutes later he reined in beside them. Dixon introduced Billy Flint, who nodded but did not speak.

"They told me at the *casa* that you were down this way," Sherwood said to Dixon. "Wanted to talk to you, so I rode down in hope of running into you."

"What's on your mind, Craig?" Dixon asked.

"This," said Sherwood. "I gather you're figuring to roll a shipping herd before long?" Dixon nodded.

"Well," said Sherwood, "as perhaps you know, I'm short-handed right now—nothing new about that. I'm trying to get a small herd together myself. I can do that, but I don't like to run the critters north with the few hands I got. So I was wondering if I could join my drive with yours?"

"No reason why you shouldn't that I can see," Dixon agreed.

"Funny things been happening in this valley of late," Sherwood explained his request. "I sure can't afford to lose a bunch of cows right now. My stuff is good, as you know, and might prove sort of tempting to gents with share-the-wealth notions. The Robertses said they lost more cows night before last," he added with apparent irrelevance.

Dixon's eyes narrowed, but Sherwood broke in before he could speak.

"I know what you're thinking, Val. But did it ever occur to you that there are gents down to the south of here who are sort of prone to wide-looping cows? Stolen cattle were run through that canyon and south by way of Bleached Bones Trail long before the Robertses ever showed up in this section, according to what Granddad used to say. No reason why it couldn't be done now. And they'd have to pass over your land to run 'em through the canyon."

"Well, they won't—" Flint began. A quick glance from Dixon stopped him. Billy, whose perceptions were hair-trigger acute, deftly changed what he was going to say to—"be swaggering around town and sounding off so loud this time, after what happened last week."

Sherwood, who evidently hadn't noticed the bit of byplay, nodded his head in agreement.

"I've a notion you're right," he said. "Blount Roberts got a lesson he isn't liable to forget for a while. But what I wanted to say is that the Roberts bunch may really have been losing cows. And if they have, the rest of us better keep our eyes open. That's the way I feel about it, and that's why I don't like to run my herd north short-handed like I am."

"No reason why you can't go along with us," Dixon repeated.

"Much obliged, Val," Sherwood said. "I'll start my boys hustling right away and we'll be ready when you are."

They came abreast of the Cross W ranch-house. Dixon and Flint turned off. Sherwood, with a wave of the hand, rode on.

CHAPTER FIVE

SEVERAL BUSY DAYS followed, with everybody combing and checking and tallying in an effort to get together the very best beef on the Cross W for shipment. Dixon was fully occupied from morning till night and had no time to think of anything else.

Finally, confident that the shipping herd was progressing in a satisfactory manner, he holed up one morning in the little room he called his office to take care of neglected book work. Turner and the hands were all up on the east pasture rooting hide-aways out of the draws and canyons which scored the hills to the south.

Dixon completed the tedious chore, had a cup of coffee and walked out into the sunshine.

Getting the rig on Rojo, he rode west by south at a moderate pace, watchful and alert, studying the distant slopes and every grove and thicket.

The ride was a long one, and several hours had elapsed when he saw the horseman riding west near the base of the southern hills. Instantly he redoubled his vigilance, his eyes never leaving the shadowy rider who appeared to be pacing him, as he neither pulled ahead nor fell back. He knew he must be clearly visible to the other, being in the full flood of the sunshine.

He glanced ahead and estimated that he was still a little more than two miles from the end wall of the valley. Another glance told him that the mysterious

33

horseman was still riding parallel to the course he followed and really keeping pace with him.

"Well, we'll find out about that," he told Rojo. Veering the sorrel's head more to the south, he quickened his gait a bit. And very quickly he realized that his shadow over there amid the shadows had also speeded up.

"Sift sand, feller," he told Rojo. "The Hellion will have either to try and ride up the slope or turn north. Either way we can come up with him. Let's go!"

Rojo bounded forward, Dixon, his glance on the rider to the south, saw that he, too, was urging his mount to top speed. The race was on!

Slowly but surely the big sorrel closed the gap. The thousand yards shrank to seven hundred, to six-fifty, to six hundred. Dixon smiled grimly. The devil didn't have a chance.

Suddenly the distant rider twisted in the saddle. Dixon saw a puff of smoke and almost at the same instant heard the whine of a slug passing overhead. He decided to show the other that he could mean business also. Knotting the split reins, he let them fall on Rojo's neck, knowing that he could guide the sorrel by knee pressure. Sliding his Winchester from the boot, he cocked it, threw it to his shoulder and let fly, aiming well above the other's head. The rider ducked, bent forward. For the next few minutes there was hard riding on the part of both.

But now the western cliffs were close. The quarry would have to turn or tackle the slope. He did turn, racing north almost in the shadow of the cliffs. Following the short leg of the triangle, Rojo was swiftly overhauling him.

Once more a twist in the saddle, once more a puff of smoke, and once more a whine of a bullet, this time uncomfortably close. Dixon flung the Winchester to his shoulder and set another "suggestion" that the other should halt and surrender, aiming slightly in front of the roan's nose and low down. He saw the bullet kick up a spurt of dust under the flying horse's front feet. Then he swore angrily at himself. He had forgotten the canyon scoring the south slope close to the west wall. Apparently his quarry hadn't, for he swerved sharply and vanished into the gloomy gorge. But unless somebody had cleared away the rock fall, he might well find himself blocked, or at least slowed up enough to enable his pursuer to overhaul him.

Into the canyon Dixon thundered. Ahead he spotted his quarry; Rojo had gained still more. He gripped his rifle firmly, debating whether to try another shot that might cause the other to halt, and decided against it for the time being. The distance was still rather great for accurate firing, and he didn't want to kill the devil and by doing so shut his mouth for good.

A mile was covered, the best part of another, with Rojo still gaining on the roan, but more slowly now, for the going was rough. The fugitive reached the bend beyond which was the rock fall, flashed around it and out of sight. Dixon slowed Rojo's pace. If the other holed up amid the fallen rocks he might be in a position to give his pursuer a hot reception. As he neared the bend, he slowed the sorrel still more and rounded it almost at a walk, his rifle ready for instant action. Then he swore. Somebody *had* cleared the trail; the fragments of stone had been tumbled into the river. And the fugitive had got another head start.

Dixon's voice rang out—"Trail, Rojo, trail!" The great sorrel snorted and proceeded to give his all. He slugged his head above the bit, blew through his flaring nostrils and literally poured his long body over the ground, his steely legs shooting back like piston rods. Steadily he closed the gap, and when at last the roan shot from the south mouth of the canyon and onto the grassy plateau, Rojo was less than three hundred yards behind him. And when the golden horse cleared the canyon, the three hundred had shrunk to not much more than two hundred.

Again the roan's rider twisted in the saddle. Dixon swayed sideways as the rifle spoke, but just the same he felt the lethal breath of the passing lead.

"All right, that does it!" he growled. He clamped the Winchester to his shoulder. The front sight dropped slowly into the rear sight's notch, down and down. Dixon was aiming a bit to the right, hoping for a shoulder wound that would knock the other from the saddle, but wouldn't necessarily be fatal. Dixon held his breath and squeezed the trigger.

And at that instant the roan fell, flinging his rider from the hull like a stone from a slingshot. Over and over went the horse in a prodigious somersault. He struck the ground with a thud; his legs jerked spasmodically for a moment and went still. The rider also lay prone on the grass without sound or motion.

The motionless form suddenly twisted over sideways and drew a gun. Dixon leaped forward and kicked. The toe of his boot caught the gun on the lock and sent it flying. He reached down, gripped the other by the shirt front and jerked him erect. Then his body went rigid and he stared incredulously.

The rider's broad-brimmed hat had flown off, revealing a mop of curly hair the colour of a forest pool brimful of sunset. Wide, frightened blue eyes met his.

"Let me go!" the girl cried. "Take your hands off me!"

A blaze of furious anger swept over Val Dixon— anger directed at her because of what had so nearly happened, what *would* have happened if the roan hadn't chosen that miraculously opportune instant to stumble and fall.

"I'll take my hands off you!" he roared. He swung her through the air and across his knee and proceeded to administer a good old-fashioned spanking.

She squalled as his hand rose and fell with rhythmic force. "Stop it!" she screamed. "Stop it!"

Dixon spanked the harder!

She was whimpering now between each yelp as the hand descended. "Please!" she cried. "Please stop! You're killing me! Oh, please! Please! Please!"

Dixon jerked her erect and slammed her on her feet with a force that clicked her teeth together.

She faced him, weeping with pain and rage, her blue eyes blazing. But as her gaze took in his tall form, her expression grew speculative. Silently Val fumbled paper and tobacco from his shirt pocket and began rolling a cigarette with fingers that shook a little.

"Could you spare me one?" the girl asked composedly. "I feel I could stand a whiff about now."

Still silent, Dixon handed her the completed brain tablet and touched a match to it. Then he rolled one for himself, lighted it, drew in a deep lungful of smoke and found his voice.

"What did you mean by throwing lead at me?" he demanded. "And who the devil are you, anyhow?"

She ignored the first question, answered the second. "I'm Rosalee Roberts."

"I might have known it!" he growled. "I've heard about you, you red-haired spitfire!"

"You haven't exactly a lamb-like disposition yourself," she retorted. "Who are *you*?"

Dixon told her. The big eyes widened a little.

"You're the man who very nearly killed my cousin, Blount Roberts," she stated rather than asked.

"That's right," Dixon admitted.

Her eyes surveyed his scarred face. "I see he left his mark on you," she said. "Rather becoming though. Gives you a nice ferocious look. With a red handkerchief over your hair, a beard and a cutlass, you'd look just as I've always imagined Jean Lafitte, the Gulf pirate, looked."

"Nice comparison!" he snorted.

"Oh, Lafitte wasn't so bad," she countered. "I understand he also had a way with women."

"Also?"

The red lips twitched a little, as if in a repressed smile, and the light in her eyes seemed to dance. Otherwise she paid no heed to his bewildered question.

"My poor horse," she said. "I'm afraid he's done for."

"Busted his neck," Dixon replied. "A wonder you didn't bust yours, too. You aren't hurt?" He tried to keep any trace of anxiety out of his voice, and failed signally.

This time she really did smile, with a flash of white, even little teeth.

"Not by the fall," she said, indulging in a surreptitious rub.

Dixon experienced a twinge of remorse. "Perhaps I shouldn't have walloped you so hard," he said, "but I figured you had it coming."

"Perhaps I did," was her surprising admission. "I suppose I shouldn't have lost my head and taken a shot at you, but you scared me when you took after me that way. Strange things have been happening in this valley of late. Why did you do it? Do you always go for folks who just happen to ride across your holding?"

Dixon hesitated, then told her, in detail. "So you see I'm a bit suspicious of anybody riding along in the shadow of the hills," he concluded.

"And I suppose you blame my cousins for what happened," she said.

"Isn't it natural that I should?" he countered.

"I suppose it is, from your viewpoint," she replied.

"But not from yours?"

Her eyes met his. "I don't know," she admitted frankly. "The boys are wild and reckless and headstrong, but somehow I can't see them going in for deliberate cold-blooded murder."

"Blount Roberts figured to kill me when he challenged me to that knife duel," Dixon pointed out.

"Yes, but he knew he was taking a chance, and took it. Blowing a cliff down on a man's head is different."

"Somewhat," he agreed dryly. "Well, I've got to figure how to get you home. We'll take the rig off your horse and tie it on behind my hull. Rojo will pack it. But I'm afraid I'll have to carry you in front of me."

"That will be all right," she said. "I'm hardly in shape to sit a saddle right now."

The sun was low in the west when they reached the Cross W ranch-house, but nobody was around except the old Mexican cook, who bobbed and smiled and asked no questions.

"Nothing can surprise Estaban," Dixon said as he dismounted. "If the sky fell, he'd just smile and go about his business. I'll rig you a critter after a bit, but first we'll have a cup of coffee and a snack. I'm hungry, and I don't doubt you are, too."

"I'm starved," she admitted.

Estaban took care of Rojo and then busied himself in the kitchen. Rosalee, who was familiar with the layout of the ranch-house, having visited it often before the death of old Salmon Walsh, cuddled up comfortably in an easy chair that had a soft cushion.

"I think I'll take it along with me when I leave," she said. "The prospect of a saddle still doesn't appeal."

They were at table when Bob Turner, Billy Flint and several more of the cowboys entered. The punchers stared in polite surprise, and when Dixon gravely introduced his guest, their astonishment was comical.

Rosalee, however, sat serene, completely mistress of the situation. She had a smile and a pleasant word for each, and apparently did not notice their bewilderment.

Later, after she had ridden away on the borrowed horse Dixon had saddled and bridled with his own hands, old Bob Turner shook his head.

"She's got red hair like the rest of 'em," he muttered, "and I've a notion she's got a temper, too; all redheaded gals have. John Cooley said she was a ridin', shootin' tomboy, but there sure ain't nothing boyish about that shape of hers. She's a looker! Val, how in blazes did you tie onto her?"

Dixon told them, refraining from mentioning the spanking episode. Turner swore. Billy Flint grinned his crooked grin. The others mumbled their amazement.

"And so you came nigh to pluggin' her," observed Turner.

"Just a miracle that I didn't," Dixon replied, his voice strained. "My front sight was dead on her back when her horse took a header. Starts me sweating even to think about it."

"I don't wonder," said Turner. "Val, you've always been full of surprises of one sort or another, but I guess you'll never beat this one. Wonder what the Robertses will say when they hear about it?"

"I don't know and I don't give a hoot," Dixon replied, "And I don't think she will, either. She won't take any pushing around."

"You can say that double," grunted Turner. "I've a notion it would go hard with any man who laid a hand on her, or even tried to talk rough to her, for that matter."

Dixon was silent, and bit back a grin with difficulty.

The shipping herd rolled up to Lenton shortly after noon the following day. The cows were held on pasture about a mile outside the town. Dixon and Bob Turner rode in to interview the buyer who had expressed his willingness to handle the shipment. They located his office, next to a saloon, dismounted and, after knocking and receiving a jovial invitation to come in, entered and found themselves face to face with Mr. Nate Billings, the buyer, who sat in a swivel chair behind a desk, smoking a cigar.

Mr. Billings had a fleshy face, blue-black where it was shaven, shifty eyes and nicked teeth.

"How are you, Mr. Dixon?" he said. "What can I do for you?"

"Well, my herd is just outside of town, waiting for your word to weigh in and drive to the loading pens, Dixon told him.

"Ah, yes, the shipping herd," said Mr. Billings, rolling his cigar from one corner of his mouth to the other. "I greatly regret to inform you, Mr. Dixon, that circumstances have arisen that make it impossible for me to handle that herd."

"Impossible to handle it!" Dixon repeated in astonishment. "But you assured me you would handle it and be glad to."

"Ah, yes," replied Billings, "But that was before I received instructions to the contrary from the main office."

"But what the devil does it mean?" demanded the bewildered ranch owner.

"I can't say," answered Mr. Billings. "All I can do is follow instructions. I'm just a buyer, you know, and don't dictate the policies of my company. Perhaps you can find another buyer."

"From what I have learned, for years your company has had a monopoly of the cattle business done in this section," Dixon said. "No other company is interested, and to contact another company and another buyer will take time and expense I can't afford."

"I'm sorry, Mr. Dixon, but that is how the situation stands," said Billings. "I can't go against my orders and contract for your herd. That's final, Mr. Dixon, and please don't blame me for something I can't help. And now, Mr. Dixon, I have a lot of work to do."

Dixon hesitated, but he could not see where anything was to be gained by prolonging the interview.

"Very well, Mr. Billings," he said, and left the office. Outside, he and Turner looked at each other blankly. Dixon broke the silence.

"Looks like we're up against real trouble, Bob," he said. "Yes, looks like my hunch was a straight one."

"But can't you get in touch with another buyer?" Turner asked.

"It's a peculiar situation here," Dixon replied. "Billings' company is a big one with lots of influence. No other outfit would care to horn in on their preserves for so insignificant a reason. After all, to a big outfit, what I ship is of little consequence. I'll try, but I'm afraid it'll be no use. Our only alternative is to make a long drive clear out of the section to some place where we can dispose of the cows, which will cost us plenty in lost beef weight and other things. Looks like the Robertses have scored, Bob."

"Yes, it looks that way," Turner agreed, adding grimly, "and I predict that before all is done I'll shoot me a Roberts or two. Come on; let's get a drink and something to eat and then talk things over. I noticed a place a little way up the street that looked all right, and it's got a name that just fits the way I feel right now—'The Widow Maker.' Only I gather none of the Roberts are married except old Clanton, and he's a widower. Come along before I bust a cinch."

The rode up the street, which ran east and west, to the saloon in question, hitched their horses at a convenient rack and pushed their way through the swinging doors.

CHAPTER SIX

MR. NATE BILLINGS was sprawled in his chair, complacently smoking a fresh cigar, when the door opened without a knock and a girl entered. Not even the dust and travel stains of a sixty-mile ride were able to detract from her the amazing good looks, and there were jewel points of light in her blue eyes that an artist would have given a year of his life to catch upon a canvas. And anybody well acquainted with Miss Rosalee Roberts would have instantly hunted cover.

Mr. Billings floundered to his feet and bowed, though his body was not formed to bend that way.

"Miss Roberts!" he exclaimed. "This is indeed an honour."

Rosalee walked across the room to face him. She did not raise her voice when she spoke, but her words struck with the impact of bullets.

"Sit down!" she said. "Sit down, you snake-blooded skunk!"

Mr. Billings' mouth dropped open. He looked like a fish that had just been jerked from the water. "Why— why—'" he gasped, and flopped back into his chair. Rosalee stood looking at him, the jewel points even more in evidence. Mr. Billings' mouth twitched. He writhed in his chair. His cigar dropped to the floor. Rosalee spoke again.

"What do you mean by refusing to buy Val Dixon's cattle?" she demanded.

"Why—why—" stuttered Mr. Billings. "The main office—"

"You're a dirty, contemptible liar," Rosalee said. "You got no such orders from the main office."

"I have to act in the best interests of my company," gulped Mr. Billings. "I—"

"You act in what you think is the best interest of your pocket," Rosalee interrupted. "How much did Blount pay you to take part in this low-down skulduggery?

"You know what I've a good notion to do?" she added before Mr. Billings could speak. "I've a notion to pin you to that chair with half a dozen forty-five slugs."

Her slender fingers writhed over the butt of the big Colt at her hip as she spoke. Mr. Billings went ashen.

"Please, Miss Roberts," he gasped. "Please—Blount said—"

"Blount has no right to say anything where the Walking R is concerned," she interrupted again. "He has no authority to speak for the Walking R, but I have, and I tell you what I'm going to do if you persist in going ahead with this crooked scheme. I'm going to see to it that your company never buys another head of stock from any outfit in Star Drive Valley and the surrounding country. I'll let *you* explain to your company. How much did Blount pay you?"

"He bought me a drink and—" began Mr. Billings.

"That's enough," said Rosalee. "Judas got thirty pieces of silver. I imagine your piece of betrayal wasn't much greater. Okay; see how long it will keep you eating after you're out of a job." She whirled and headed for the door.

"Wait!" bleated Mr. Billings. "Where are you going?"

"I'm going to the telegraph office and burn up the wires between here and Kansas City," Rosalee replied. "I'll get to the bottom of this business, fast. I'll find out what your company has to say about it."

"Wait!" wailed Mr. Billings, bouncing out of his chair and flopping back again when she turned to look at him. "Wait! I'll do anything you say? What do you want me to do?"

Rosalee gazed at him a moment, then returned to face him. Her fingers still toyed with the butt of her gun. Sweat streamed down his fat face. Rosalee spoke.

"Go find Mr. Dixon—I think I saw his horse standing at the rack in front of the Widow Maker when I rode into town—and tell him to start weighing his cows and shoving them into the pens or the corral. Then get back here, fast."

"I'll do it," promised Mr. Billings. He struggled out of his chair and waddled for the door.

"Wait!" said Rosalee. Mr. Billings halted, glancing apprehensively over his shoulder.

"And if you mention my name to Mr. Dixon, or a word of this conversation, I *will* shoot you," she said. "Get going!"

With a gulping sigh of relief, Mr. Billings scuttled out of the door. Rosalee sat down in his vacated chair, fished the makings from her shirt pocket and rolled a cigarette with the slender fingers of her left hand.

Rosalee was calm enough, but Mr. Billings wasn't. By the time he came to the Widow Maker and found Dixon there, he was flushed and anxious. All his fat chins were quavering with emotion and he panted until he could scarcely speak.

"Hullo!" said Turner, "Here comes trouble!"

Dixon turned and saw Billings coming through the batwings.

"What's biting him?" he asked, suspiciously. "Has he had second thoughts."

"If he has," commented Flint, "it's along of somebody prodding him with a gun——"

"Or a knife," added Turner.

Dixon watched as Billings came ambling up to him trying to conceal the fact how ill at ease he was.

"Glad I've found you, Dixon," he said. "There's been a change. I find I can buy your beasts after all."

Val watched him narrowly. "How come?" he asked.

"A rush message from main office," explained Billings. "A shipment's gone sour on them so they're needing your cows. You get the animals penned then come over to my office and we'll see about the cash. Okay?"

"Well, this is glad news," said Val. "I'll do just that, Mr. Billings."

"I'm busy," returned Billings. "You get the job done. Be seeing you."

He left the Widow Maker in a hurry, and left Val frowning with perplexity.

"It smells," murmured Val, thoughtfully. "Somebody's prodded him, like you said, Billy. Maybe we'll find out, one day, all about it, and maybe we never shall. But we'll do what he says because I sure need those dollars."

So they got the cows penned as Billings had requested, but Billings returned to his office to find Rosalee still there.

"Well, I've done it," he announced sullenly. "He'll be around soon for the dinero."

"You've got enough dollars?" she asked.

"Sure have," he admitted.

"Then pay him, or else," she threatened. "And don't worry about Blount. I'll tell him what I've done when I next see him, which may not be for some time."

She left him to think it over. When Dixon arrived Billings duly paid him the dollars due.

"Thanks," said Val. "It's too late now to hit the trail so I'll stay in town for the night. Have to hide these dollars somehow. Thanks again!"

There was a nasty glint in Billings' eyes as Val left the office.

CHAPTER SEVEN

IN HIS OFFICE, Nate Billings sat rolling his cigar between his lips and muttering under his breath. Suddenly his muddy eyes glowed. He bit hard on his cigar, his hands trembling with excitement. Drawing pen and paper from a drawer, he began to scribble words on the sheet.

Folding the sheet, he sealed it in an envelope. With trepidation, he glanced around cautiously after leaving the office, then hurried down the street and entered a dingy-looking saloon. As he expected, the man he sought was lounging at the bar, a lean, hard-faced individual with dark, watchful eyes. Billings approached him with elaborate casualness, nodded a greeting and ordered drinks for them both. After the bartender had filled the glasses and moved to the other end of the bar, Billings spoke in low tones, making sure first that nobody was within hearing distance.

"Take this letter, Jess, and get it to Blount Roberts as fast as you can ride," he said. "I think you'll find him in Muerto when you get there. Start just as soon as you finish your drink. If your horse isn't okay, you can have my dun. And, Jess—forget all about it. Here!"

The man's eyes gleamed as he read the denomination of the crisp banknote that was the price of silence.

"Okay, Nate, I'm gone," he said. He gulped his drink and sauntered from the saloon. Mr. Billings' hand shook as he raised his own glass.

Jess did not immediately ride south. Instead, he gained his room over the saloon by way of an outside stairs. He kindled a fire in a small stove and set a kettle of water on to heat. When the water came to a boil he steamed open the envelope. His eyes glowed as he read what Billings had written.

For a moment he sat in thought; then he fumbled a rubber-tipped pencil and a pen and bottle of ink from a table drawer. With the greatest care he erased a single word and did a little equally careful work with the pen, surveying the result with satisfaction.

"Guess that'll hold you in Muerto and keep you from snooping around here too soon, *Señor* Roberts," he muttered. He slipped the sheet back in the envelope, resealed it and descended the stairs.

After making sure Billings had departed, he entered the saloon and approached a squat, mottle-faced man standing at the bar.

"Come outside, Parks," he said in low tones. "I got something I want you to do; there's a sawbuck in it for you."

Outside, he handed Parks a bill and the letter. "Find Blount Roberts in Muerto and give it to him," he directed. "Don't give it to anybody else or let anybody see it. If you can't find Roberts, hang onto it till you get a chance to hand it back to me. Understand?"

"Okay," replied Parks, stowing the letter in an inside pocket. "But what about the Boss? He'll be wondering why I don't show up."

"Don't worry about the Boss; I'll see him," Jess answered.

"Okay," Parks repeated. "I'll get going right away."

Jess went back to the saloon and had a drink. Then

he left and sauntered to an even dingier saloon farther down the street. He entered, spotted a poker game and nodded significantly to one of the players, who immediately excused himself and joined Jess at a table in a far corner. For several minutes they talked earnestly. Jess arose and moseyed out. The other went back to his game.

After several hours spent at the Widow Maker, Dixon tired of the bellow of conversation and the racket in general. With quite a few drinks under his belt, he felt relaxed and comfortable. A stroll in the night air would be just the thing. Satisfied that the boys were okay, he sauntered out. He did not notice Billy Flint's eyes follow him as he passed through the swinging doors. Flint seemed to hesitate, then shrugged his shoulders and turned back to his drink. However, he kept casting glances at the door, his brows drawing together.

Outside, Lenton's night life was under way. Strains of music or what passed for it sounded from the saloons and dance halls. Dixon chuckled and walked slowly along the main street; he was liking the Big Bend country better and better.

From time to time he paused to gaze into shop windows. He entered a couple of saloons and had a drink in each. The sandwiches displayed in a little eating house attracted him and he enjoyed one in a leisurely fashion. Yes, the Big Bend country was okay.

Gradually he left the busier and better lighted section of the town behind. The quiet was pleasant, and the feel of the night wind on his face. He slowed his pace still more, busy with his thoughts. He must be nearing the place where Sherwood had said he'd be holed up in a poker game. Might be a good notion to see a few hands.

Sherwood had said the place was quiet. He strolled on slowly. A little distance ahead was a gleam of light filtering through windows badly in need of washing. It was just beyond the mouth of a narrow, dark alley. He was moseying past the alley when he sensed movement in the shadows. A warning signal sounded in his brain an instant too late. The movement amid the shadows was behind him. He didn't need to be told that what was suddenly jammed against his back was the steely muzzle of a gun.

"Just keep on walking, slow," said a voice over his shoulder. "Don't try nothing or you'll get it."

Dixon obeyed; there was nothing else to do. There were two men behind him, one pressing the gun muzzle against his back, the other a little to the right. From the corner of his eye he could just make out a bulky figure and a bearded face.

With Dixon pacing slowly, his captors keeping step, they passed a dingy little saloon through the dirty windows of which seeped the glow of light. Two more strides and they reached a corner.

"Turn left," said the voice of the gun wielder. "Easy now!"

Dixon turned jerkily. He felt the gun muzzle slide along his back to the right, and went sideways and down. He gasped as the gun boomed and the slug tore along his ribs. Then he was on the ground, rolling over and over.

A bullet knocked dirt into his face. Another ripped the sleeve of his shirt. He drew with his left hand and fired again and again. Answering shots slammed the ground beside him, close. Then he saw one of the gunmen crumple up like a sack of old clothes. He fired again, and the second man raised himself on his tiptoes, reeling back to fall and lie in a crumpled heap.

Dixon strove to regain his feet and could not. The best he could essay was a sitting position. Blood was soaking his shirt. His right side was a flame of pain. His gun dropped from his nerveless fingers to thud softly in the dust.

From the saloon sounded startled yells, and a pounding of boots on the boards. Men streamed out, shouting questions. They grouped beside the two bodies, staring at Dixon. A voice rang out:

"Hey! this is Jess Willoughby! That feller there must have killed him!"

A mutter ran through the crowd. "He was a good feller, Jess. Yes, Jess was all right. We ain't going to stand for anything like this being done to Jess."

Dixon knew the mob had him at its mercy, but he was too weak and sick and pain-racked to care. Vaguely he felt he should reach for his remaining gun and shoot it out with the hellions, but the effort was too great. His numbed mind refused to countenance such exertion.

"Guess we'd better get a rope," somebody said.

"I guess you'd better not," said a voice behind the group, a deep and harsh and growling voice that should have come from the throat of a giant. It didn't. It came from the lips of a slender, boyish-looking fellow who stared at the would-be lynchers with pale, cold eyes.

The mob turned to face Billy Flint, who lounged easily on widespread feet, the thumbs of his slender hands hooked over his double cartridge belts and just above the black gun buts flaring out from his sinewy hips.

One of the hands moved like a striking rattler, a mere

formless blur. Flame and smoke gushed from his side. A man who had stealthily drawn a gun went down, screaming hoarsely and clutching at his bullet-smashed hand. The gun, one butt plate knocked off, lay a dozen feet distant. Flint's voice blared at the others:

"Up! Get your hands up! The next one won't be through a fist! Up!"

There was a gun in each of the slender hands now, and those terrible pale eyes seemed to single out each man of the mob for individual attention.

The hands went up, a forest of them, reaching for the stars. Billy Flint took three catlike steps backwards.

"All right," he said. "Back in that rumhole you came out of, and stay there. Move!"

They moved slowly and cautiously, lest some gesture be misinterpreted by the icy-eyed young devil who stood glaring at them. The doors swung on the last.

Dixon had managed to gather a little strength; he picked up his fallen gun and got to his feet, to stand weaving, the cocked gun in his hand.

"All right; come on across while I watch the door," said Flint. "Never mind those two skunks; they're done for. Good shooting, Val!"

Dixon tried not to look down at the dead faces as he passed the bodies, but they drew his eyes like a lodestone. He gulped a deep and shuddering breath. At last he was a killer, and he didn't like it. Another instant and he was beside Flint, both of them backing away from the door and the lighted windows.

One of Flint's guns blazed. A scream of pain and a volley of curses echoed the report.

"That one who tried to look out of the door knows I

wasn't fooling," Billy remarked. "Got him square in the middle. Hope he dies sweatin'."

Dixon shuddered again. The cold killer by his side was rather terrible, even as a staunch friend.

"Let's go," he muttered. "I don't think any more of them will show."

"Okay," said Flint. He holstered one gun and flung an arm around Dixon's waist, bolstering his shambling steps. "To the Widow Maker," he added. "The boys are all there, and you need a little fixing up. Losing much blood?"

"I think it's slackening," Dixon replied. "Really nothing but a scrape along my ribs, but the shock was terrific. I'm getting stronger. Believe I can walk by myself."

"You won't try it just yet," said Flint.

"How come you happened along at just the right time?" Dixon asked, still leaning heavily on Flint's arm.

"I got bothered when you left the saloon, and when you didn't show for quite a while I got more bothered," Billy explained. "So I decided to go looking for you. Heard the shooting and figured you might be in trouble; so I hightailed down the street. Guess I was right."

"You were, definitely," Dixon said. "Here come some folks."

People were approaching, but cautiously. Apparently too impulsive an investigation of a Lenton shooting might prove unhealthy.

"Hey, who's that?" Flint exclaimed.

A compact body of men had burst through the straggling crowd and was headed down the street almost at a run.

"It's the boys," chuckled Flint. "They must have

heard something off-colour was going on. Look at 'em hightail!"

The Cross W cowboys surged up to Dixon and Flint, volleying questions.

"What happened, Val?" demanded Bob Turner.

Dixon told him briefly as he paused to rest a moment. Others were crowding close to listen.

"Must have happened right outside the Last Chance," somebody remarked. "That rumhole is always full of owlhoots."

Turner's face set like stone. "Come on, boys," he said quietly. We'll clean that place from one end to the other, and hang everybody left alive by his whiskers. Come on!"

"Hold it!" Dixon told him. "There've been enough killings for one night; I don't want any more. Besides, there's no proof the bunch in that saloon had anything to do with it. They came out after the shooting was over."

Several members of the crowd jeered derisively. "Jess Willoughby was one of 'em, eh?" said a voice. "That shiftless skunk always held out in there. Let your boys go, feller."

"No," Dixon said. "Come on; we're heading back to the Widow Maker so I can get strapped up. My side doesn't feel too good."

The lust for vengeance on the part of the Cross W punchers turned to anxiety as to Dixon's condition. Without argument they trooped along behind him and Flint.

"I'm really feeling a lot better, but I figured that would get them in line," Dixon remarked in low tones to Billy. "No sense in looking for trouble."

"Sometimes," Billy grunted. "Then sometimes it ain't so. I got a feeling this is one of the times."

Somebody had run ahead with the story of what had happened, and when they arrived at the Widow Maker, Swayback Sawyer, the proprietor, was all set for business.

"Right into the back room with him," he directed. "I'm used to patchin' up punctured gents. Got bandages, salve, cloths and water ready and waiting. Right this way, Mr. Dixon; I'll have you restin' easy in a jiffy."

He beckoned to Flint, Turner and a couple more of the Cross W hands.

"The rest of you stay out here," he directed. "I don't want you clutterin' up the room and disturbin' the patient. Everybody else out, I say."

The order was obeyed, for Swayback was a tough old customer when crossed.

When the door was closed, he seated Dixon in a chair, deftly removed his shirt and disclosed a ragged furrow scoring the flesh over his lower ribs.

"Nothin' to it," he rumbled. "Just a scratch, but must have hit you one devil of a lick. Knocked the wind out of you and turned your stomach upside down, eh?"

"Just about," Dixon admitted.

Swayback went to work with water, soothing ointment and bandages. "I'd make a better doctor than most sawbones." He chuckled as he patted a final padding and bandage into place. "Get lots of experience in the likker business. There, that ought to hold you."

The door swung open. Swayback let out a wrathful bellow.

"Didn't I say I didn't want anybody comin'—Oh!"

hello, Miss Roberts! Come right in and shut the door."
Rosalee banged the door in the faces of those peering
after her and walked forward. Her eyes were blazing,
her fingers coiled about the butt of the forty-five swinging at her hip. "Who was responsible for this?" she
demanded harshly.

"Don't worry about them, ma'am," replied Billy
Flint. "Val took care of them, proper."

Rosalee turned to Dixon. "Just what did happen?"
she asked.

Dixon told her. Her eyes grew thoughtful.

"And you figure they just intended to rob you?"

"Looked that way to me," Dixon answered. "I don't
think they were out to kill me unless they had to. Otherwise they would have handled it differently. I'd say
their plan was to shove me down that dark street on
the other side of the saloon, clean me and let me go."

"Maybe," said Billy Flint. "*Los muertos no hablan.*"

"Yes," translated Rosalee, "the dead do not talk. If
I could only be sure," she added cryptically, seemingly
to herself.

The door opened again. A plump and pompous
individual bustled in. On his shirt front he wore a big
nickel badge. He glowered at Dixon disapprovingly.

"Hear tell you just killed three fellers," he said in
accusing tones. "I don't stand for that in my town.
Guess I'll have to—"

"Shut up!" Rosalee blazed at him. "Did you see him
kill somebody?"

"Why—why, no—" the town marshal began.

"Did *anybody* see him kill somebody?" Rosalee
persisted.

The marshal hemmed and hawed. "Why, I guess

not," he admitted. "But the boys at the Last Chance said—"

"You heard! They said!" Rosalee interrupted with withering scorn. "Get out! Get out before I have the boys throw you out. Get out, I say!"

The marshal got out.

Rosalee turned on Dixon. "And as for you," she stormed, "I can't leave you alone an hour but you go and get yourself into trouble!"

"I wasn't doing anything," Dixon protested.

"No! You weren't doing anything! Just prowling around the dark streets by yourself! Come along! You're going to the hotel and to bed. Come along, I say!"

"Yes, ma'am," Dixon replied meekly, and followed her out of the door.

The Cross W hands looked at one another. Bob Turner broke the silence.

"Gents," he said sententiously, "I've a notion we're going to end up working for a Boss what is a Boss."

"And a gal to ride the river with," added Billy Flint.

CHAPTER EIGHT

WHEN DIXON AWOKE to sunshine pouring through the window, his side was still sore, but the stabbing pain had ceased and he felt a great deal better.

Dressing was something of a chore because of the stiffness and soreness of his side and arm, but he finally accomplished it and headed for the Widow Maker for something to eat. He pushed through the swinging doors and paused, his eyes narrowing slightly.

Seated at a table were Rosalee Roberts and Craig Sherwood, engrossed in conversation.

Rosalee happened to look up. She saw Dixon hesitating at the door and waved her hand.

"Come and join us," she called. "We're waiting for our orders. Hope you're hungry as I am. How do you feel this morning?"

"Okay," Dixon replied shortly. He hesitated to accept the invitation but decided it would be ungracious not to do so. Sherwood stood up and drew out a chair.

"Save you any unnecessary exertion," he smiled. "From what I heard about last night, you're lucky to be able to feel at all."

"Guess that's so," Dixon agreed as he sat down, Sherwood solicitously pushing the chair forward. Rosalee's red lips twitched and Dixon read amusement in her eyes.

During the meal, Craig Sherwood monopolized the

conversation. He had an easy flow of speech, was witty and entertaining. Dixon felt awkward and inarticulate in comparison. He said little, and directed his attention to his food. From time to time he stole a glance at Rosalee. It seemed to him the colour in her cheeks was more vivid and added sparkle to her eyes. There was no doubt but that she found Sherwood interesting.

Finally breakfast came to an end, to Dixon's relief. Abruptly he had a decided longing to be elsewhere. He rose to his feet.

"Well, I'm heading back for the spread," he said. "Coming, Craig?"

"I'll be along later," Sherwood replied airily. "My boys will go with you."

"Just as you say," Dixon said. "So long, Miss Roberts."

"Goodbye, Mr. Dixon," Rosalee answered without turning her head, and went on talking to Sherwood.

Dixon stalked out of the door in anything but a good temper. Once outside, he paused, irresolute. Belatedly he remembered that the day before he had ordered the boys to gather at the Widow Maker for the trip home. Very shortly they would arrive, wondering where the devil he was. Well, they could wait a bit.

With a muttered oath he headed down the street.

Soon he reached the dingy saloon in front of which he had very nearly got his come-uppance the night before. In sheer bravado he entered, walked to the bar and ordered a drink. Nobody paid the least attention to him. He downed his drink, glowered about and walked out. There was not even any turning of heads as he passed through the swinging doors. Decidedly, he had missed fire. Feeling foolish, he turned and retraced his steps to the Widow Maker.

The boys were there, and so were Craig Sherwood's hands. Sherwood himself and Rosalee Roberts were conspicuous by their absence.

"Well, what do you say?" asked Bob Turner. "Feel up to riding?"

"The sooner the better," Dixon replied morosely. Turner eyed him with concern.

"You don't sound so good," he said. "Maybe we'd better wait another day."

"We won't," Dixon replied shortly. "We're leaving, right now. Is the chuck wagon ready to roll?"

"Just waiting for you to give the word," Turner answered.

"Let's go," said Dixon. "I'll meet you outside in ten minutes and we'll ride."

He repaired to the stable where his horse was quartered, got the rig on and swung into the hull, wincing a little as his sore ribs protested against undue activity. Once his feet were settled in the stirrups, however, the pain lessened and was scarcely noticeable by the time he joined the hands at the Widow Maker hitchracks. The outfit swept out of town at a good pace, the wagon lumbering after the cowboys, with old Estaban, the cook, squalling jovial profanity at his horses in half a dozen languages.

As they rode through a world all glorious with morning, Dixon's mood lightened. Billy Flint, who had been watching him anxiously, looked relieved. Dixon caught his eye and grinned.

"Sure, I'm all right," he answered the unspoken question in Flint's eyes. "Side hardly smarts at all.

Really, it wasn't more than a scratch. Shock knocked me loco for a bit, but that's worn off. Everything considered, it's been a darn good trip."

"Turned out well," Flint agreed. "Didn't look so good for a while, though."

"All's well that ends well," Dixon replied cheerfully.

"That Roberts gal sure was worked up last night," Billy Flint remarked irrelevantly. "She seemed plumb bothered about your condition."

"Just common humanity, I imagine," Dixon replied.

"Maybe," Flint conceded in a voice that did not carry conviction. "She said something that has me sort of puzzled. I wish I knew just what she meant. Said it like she was talking to herself. I don't think you heard her, but I was standing right beside her and I did."

"What did she say?" Dixon asked curiously.

"She said, 'If I could only be sure.' Now what the devil *did* she mean?"

Dixon shook his head and did not attempt to answer.

"Wonder if she's leaving town this morning?" Flint said.

"Hard to tell," Dixon replied shortly.

"Thought maybe she'd ride with us," Billy Flint pursued.

"What she chooses to do or not to do is her affair," Dixon answered shortly.

"I'd sort of hoped she would," Billy rambled on. "She's nice to have around. Would be nice to have around if the going got tough, too, I'll bet. I've a notion if that fool town marshal had hung around another minute last night, she'd have tossed him out herself instead of having us do it. Did you see the look in her eyes when she told him to get outa there? They were a lot different when they looked at you, though."

Dixon found himself wavering between laughter and exasperation. Circumstances being what they were, the frankness of Billy Flint's remarks was embarrassing. He racked his brains for some means of shutting him up. However, Billy was off on another track.

"Wonder how those two sidewinders who tried to rob you last night knew you were packing all that money on you?" he said.

"I imagine one of the boys must have talked out of turn and what he said was overheard by the wrong pair of ears," Dixon replied.

"I'll bet my last peso that nobody did," Flint declared positively. "We'd talked it over before you came in and agreed that everybody would keep a tight latigo on his jaw. Who all knew you were packing the money?"

"Only Billings, the buyer, so far as I know," Dixon replied, refraining from mentioning that Rosalee Roberts also was aware of the fact. He definitely did not want Billy to return to the subject of Miss Roberts.

The cowboy's brows knit. "Could that fat hellion have had something to do with it?" he wondered.

"Rather far-fetched to think that he did," Dixon answered. "Of course, he might have inadvertently mentioned the matter to somebody, through whom the word got around. He certainly didn't strike me as the sort who would go in for armed robbery."

"Me neither," Flint conceded, "but you never can tell. Well, somehow the word got around and those two hellions very nearly got away with it. If you didn't think as fast as you pull, they would have. Wish I'd seen the beginning of that shindig; must have been worth watching. Down on the ground, and you got 'em both dead centre! That was shooting! And you sure took a chance when you slid sideways against that gun muzzle. Fast thinking, fast shooting, and cold nerve. Gentlemen, hush!"

Flint paused to gaze admiringly at his employer.

"What I did or didn't do wouldn't have meant much if you hadn't happened along when you did," Val said. "I was all set to be the chief attraction at a necktie party. Those devils would have strung me up, sure as blazes."

"Chances are it was just talk," the cowboy said. "And it didn't take much to make a bunch of souses back down. They were all too drunk to shoot straight, even if they'd had the nerve to try it."

"One tried it and lost part of his gun hand," Dixon pointed out.

"Oh, the chances are he was just reaching for his tobacco and got hold of his gun handle by mistake," Billy replied. "If I hadn't been so jumpy and had taken a second to think, I wouldn't have plugged him."

Dixon smiled and was silent.

For several miles they rode without speaking, each busy with his own thoughts, while the Cross T hands joked and skylarked. Finally Flint inquired, "Going to lay over in Muerto for the night?"

"Yes, I think so," Dixon replied. "I'll want to deposit the money in the bank tomorrow. No sense in riding clear down to the spread and back. Also, it'll give you boys a chance for another night in town. I'm going to hand out a little bonus for you to celebrate with."

"You're a good man to work for Val," Billy chuckled. "We all appreciate it."

Another period of silence followed. Then :

"Thought Sherwood would have caught up with us by now," Flint remarked. "His boys said he'd be along shortly. Betcha he got drunk."

Dixon's answer was a grunt. Several times he glanced over his shoulder, but the Forked S owner did not put in an appearance.

When they reached Muerto, just after sundown, they found the town full of cowhands, for it was pay day at the neighbouring ranches and everybody was in for a bust.

"Going to be a wild and woolly night," Bob Turner predicted, a look of pleased anticipation in his eyes.

"Yes, I've a notion it is," agreed Dixon. "Try and stick together as much as you can," he cautioned his men. "It's the kind of night when anything could happen."

After caring for their horses, the Cross W hands and Sherwood's headed for the Silver Rail. The boys bellied up to the bar, which was already crowded. Dixon decided something to eat first was in order. He was just finishing his meal when three men entered and, after glancing around, approached his table. The foremost, a pleasant-faced, elderly man, was Judd Worthington, the president of the Muerto bank, whom Dixon knew well. The others he recognized as deputy sheriffs.

"Hello, Mr. Dixon," Worthington said. "I'd appreciate it if you could spare the time to walk to my office in the bank. Something I'd like to talk to you about."

Wonderingly, Dixon nodded agreement. His surprised hands watched him pass out of the door in company of the bank president and the deputies.

"Now what the devil!" exclaimed Billy Flint. "Are

they going to give Val trouble because of that shooting last night?"

"I doubt it," replied Bob Turner. "Chances are Worthington just wants to talk to him about some business matter."

"But why the deputies?" Flint asked, his eyes seeming to grow paler.

"I don't know," Turner was forced to admit.

When they reached the bank, Worthington unlocked the front door and ushered Dixon and the deputies in. After locking the door behind them, he led the way to his private office, the door of which stood ajar, letting out a beam of light.

"Go right in, Mr. Dixon," he invited. The deputies paused outside.

Dixon pushed the door open, and halted, staring.

Seated beside the president's desk, shapely legs comfortably crossed, was a small feminine figure.

"So you got him all right, Judd," Rosalee remarked. "As I told you, he's got the price of that big herd he sold strapped around his waist, and he hasn't enough sense to be left running around with all that money in a town like this one."

"Guess that's so," agreed the president, a grin twitching at the corners of his mouth. Dixon gulped.

"Just step behind the partition, *Mister* Dixon, and shuck off that belt," Rosalee directed. "It's going into the vault for safekeeping. You and the deputies pass the word around that it's there, Judd. Perhaps that will make him comparatively safe tonight."

Dixon gulped again, tried to speak, and couldn't summon words appropriate to the occasion. The grin spread clear across the bank president's face. The deputies lounging outside the door chuckled.

"Better do what the lady says, Mr. Dixon," Worthington advised.

"Otherwise I'll have the deputies lock you and the belt both up for the night," Rosalee added.

"Appears the Roberts family runs everything in this section," Dixon couldn't resist saying.

The president smilingly shook his head. "The Roberts family does not run the Muerto bank," he stated with finality. "However, I have always found Rosalee to be of sound judgment, and any suggestion made by her merits serious consideration. When she laid the facts of the case before me, I agree with her that it would be unwise for you to pack that money around with you tonight, especially after what happened at Lenton. There may be others of whom you know nothing mixed up in that business, and a second try might be more successful than the first."

"You win," Dixon said. He passed behind the partition and in a few moments reappeared holding the plump money belt in his hand; he passed it to the president, naming the amount it contained.

"If you wish to verify the figures, sir—" he began.

"Not necessary," the president interrupted. "Rosalee said your statement is all that's needed."

Dixon ground his teeth. "And whatever Rosalee says goes!" he snapped.

"Exactly," said the president, smiling more broadly then ever and sitting down at his desk. His pen scratched busily for a moment.

"Here's your deposit slip, Mr. Dixon," he said. He went into the bank and began twirling the combination knob of the big steel vault. The door swung open, then shut. The president returned to his office.

"Now," he said, "I think everybody feels better." He cast a questioning eye at Dixon.

"*I* do," the ranch owner admitted. "Now what?" He glanced at Rosalee, who jumped to her feet.

"Now I'm starved," she said. "Take me to the Silver Rail and buy me something to eat."

The president chuckled and looked pleased. The deputies winked at each other. Dixon suffered Miss Roberts to lead him outside.

"What became of Sherwood?" he asked.

"I haven't the slightest notion," she replied. "Getting drunk at some bar, I presume."

"I thought you'd ride together." Dixon hesitated.

"Did you?" she replied. "Why?"

"I thought—it looked like—" he stuttered.

"Appearances are sometimes deceptive," she interrupted. "Didn't you ever hear of two persons disagreeing on something?"

So that was it! They'd had a row and she was using him to take her spite out on Sherwood. Dixon's lips tightened.

CHAPTER NINE

THE STARES WHICH had greeted Rosalee when she pushed through the swinging doors of the Widow Maker in Lenton were as nothing compared to those provoked by her entrance with Val Dixon into the Silver Rail. Men at the bar forgot their glasses. Dealers froze motionless with decks of cards in their hands. The dancers faltered in their steps. Even the spinning wheels seemed to sag and slow. The babble of voices was replaced by a silence broken only by the delighted chuckle of Billy Flint.

Rosalee unconcernedly led the way to a table, waited for Dixon to pull out her chair and sat down.

"Order everything in sight; I'm famished," she told him. "You've already eaten? Well, you can have coffee or a drink while you keep me company."

"I think I'll have coffee," Dixon said weakly.

At the bar, old Bob Turner kept casting uneasy glances towards the table, a worried look in his eyes.

"This is all very nice," he muttered to Flint, "but if the Robertses and their bunch happen to walk in, there'll be a corpse-and-cartridge session here sure as blazes."

Billy shrugged. "Okay," he replied. "Bound to come sooner or later. The quicker we get it over with the better, to my way of thinking. If those hombres come looking for trouble, they'll get it."

Turner gazed around the crowded room and shook

his grizzled head. "Flying lead don't play no favourites," he pointed out. "If a row breaks, some innocent folks are liable to get hurt, including maybe some women. Lots of girls on the floor, to say nothing of the Roberts gal."

"I've a notion the Roberts gal can take care of herself," Flint said. "And the dance floor gals get paid for taking chances."

Turner, not at all convinced, shook his head again. "And *I've* a notion the Roberts gal just naturally dotes on trouble," he growled. "Look at her, laughing and making sheep's eyes at Val, and chipper as a bluejay. Nothing ever bothers her, and she's got Val not knowing which end he's standing on."

Old Bob was wrong. Rosalee *was* concerned and apprehensive, as her sudden suggestion showed.

"Let's get out of here," she said. "I like dancing and good music, and I know a little Mexican place down at the far end of the street which has both. Nice people run it. Besides, there's no sense in looking for trouble, and if some of our boys happen to drop in and see us together, there might be a row. Hardly any cowhands except from the new ranches over east go to the place I mentioned."

"But I don't like to leave my boys if trouble is liable to break," Dixon demurred.

"There won't be any trouble here," Rosalee assured him. "Our boys know better than to start a row just for the sake of starting one; it wouldn't get them anything but trouble. Sheriff Jarrett has warned them that he won't stand for any more high-handed nonsense, and they know he's very likely to be as good as his word. There's an election coming up this fall, you know, and the newcomers to the east and north can swing a lot of votes. Floyd Jarrett doesn't want them down on him, and if he allows our boys to get out of order too much, he knows that's just what will happen. But if my cousins should come and see you and me together, tempers might flare. Come on, let's get out of here."

Although still dubious, Dixon offered no further objection. Together they passed through the swinging doors and into the cool of the night under the glittering stars.

"Now where the devil are they going?" Billy Flint wondered.

"Hard to tell," replied Bob Turner, "but wherever it is, I've a notion they don't hanker for company. Let's have another drink."

Rosalee breathed deeply of the fresh night air. "Whew!" she exclaimed. "It's good to be outside after all that noise and smoke. I like the Silver Rail, but the air does get a bit thick at times. You couldn't hear yourself think!"

"My head was beginning to spin, too," Dixon admitted. "Seemed everybody was yelling at once."

"It'll be quieter where we're going," the girl said. "Lots of pretty *señoritas*, too; I've a notion you'll like it."

"Wouldn't be surprised if I do," Dixon conceded. "Do you dance?"

"I love it," she replied, "especially if I have a good partner. Do you?"

"Oh, I manage to fall over my own feet fairly gracefully," he answered.

"That's something," Rosalee said. "Most people do it clumsily."

They appeared to attract no attention as they strolled along the busy street. There were other couples, some of them town people, others from the saloons and dance halls, taking the night air, and everybody seemed intent on his or her own affairs.

Gradually they left the busier and brighter section of the town behind. Lighted windows were spaced farther apart; there were fewer people on the street. They had come almost to where the star-burned rangeland, lonely and deserted, rolled eastwards to meet the dawn, when Rosalee paused before a small building whence came strains of soft, seductive music.

"Here it is," she said: "the Quetzal."

"Named after the sacred bird of the Mayas, eh?" Dixon remarked.

"Yes, the 'Bird of Dawning,' " she replied.

"And I imagine it's still going strong at dawn," Dixon chuckled as they entered.

A smiling and bowing waiter met them, led them to a table and took their order. Dixon glanced about.

The room was bigger than it looked from the outside. Subdued lighting was provided by two hanging lamps, one over the dance floor, the other over the bar. The Mexican orchestra was good, the dance floor girls young and pretty.

"Isn't this nicer?" Rosalee asked, sipping the wine the waiter brought her.

"Anyhow, it's not so noisy," Dixon conceded. "The music is nice and the girls *are* pretty."

"Why don't you ask one to dance?" Rosalee said.

"If I dance with anyone tonight, it will be you," he replied.

"Then what are we waiting for? I like to dance."

Before the first dance was finished, she said, "You're full of surprises. I had no idea you could dance like this."

"It's easy when one has the right partner," he replied.

"That was nicely said," she answered. "Yes, I suppose anything is easy if one has the right partner," she added thoughtfully.

"It no doubt makes the hard times easier," he said. She nodded agreement.

"I think that is how life should be," she said. "Working together, knowing hardship together, finding happiness together—with the right partners."

Dixon was silent. He hardly knew how to answer, but felt there was much truth in her philosophy.

The music stopped. They returned to their table, both a little breathless, for the number had been a fast one. Dixon ordered another drink; Rosalee sipped her wine.

The orchestra began a dreamy waltz. Dixon glanced at her; she nodded and they glided onto the floor. It seemed to Val Dixon that time stood still. He was jolted back to the prosaic present when his partner suddenly stiffened in his arms.

"Good heavens!" he heard her exclaim in a low voice. "I slipped!"

He followed the gaze of her wide eyes, which were fixed on the swinging doors. They had been flung back, and two big men filled the doorway, their glances searching the room. Behind them crowded others. Dixon recognized the Roberts twins, Crane and Wilbur.

"They haven't spotted us yet," Rosalee whispered; "we've still got time."

Dixon's hand had instinctively dropped to his gun butt; but Rosalee was quicker than he. She jerked away from him. Her hand flashed down and up. Two crashing reports rocked the room, accompanied by a jangling of broken glass and splintered metal. The two hanging lamps were snuffed out. Darkness swooped down.

Instantly the room was in an uproar. Yells, curses, the screams of the dance floor girls and the thudding of overturned chairs and tables combined to create bedlam. Rosalee had Dixon by the wrist and was tugging hard.

"Come along!" she shrilled. "Follow me!"

Mechanically he obeyed, striving to shield her from figures blundering through the dark. She seemed to have eyes like a cat and steered an unerring course to the far wall of the building.

"The door!" she said. "There's a bar on it. Get it open!"

Cursing under his breath, Dixon fumbled with the bar, which rested tightly in brackets. After a struggle he got it loose and flung it aside. Rosalee jerked the door open and gave him a shove. He stumbled into the gloom of an alley back of the saloon. Rosalee darted after him and slammed the door shut.

A man loomed directly in front of them. "Gotcha!" he exclaimed.

Dixon hit him; all his muscular two hundred pounds were back of the blow. His fist grazed the fellow's jaw and hurled him sideways. He caught a gleam of metal, leaped and struck again. This time the blow connected solidly. The man went down with a queer little grunt. Dixon leaped over his body, dragging Rosalee with him. Together they fled down the alley. Behind them a gun boomed and a slug whined past. Dixon went cold.

They reached a corner. As they whipped around it, the gun blazed again. Dixon heard Rosalee gasp.

"You hit?" he cried in an agony of apprehension.

"Just ripped my sleeve," she answered. "Run!"

Another moment and they were at the main street where it ended at the edge of the prairie.

"Right across and stop in the shadow of that shed over there," said Rosalee. "Hurry!"

They reached the shed and paused in the gloom, breathless. Diagonally across the street the Quetzal was boiling like a super heated pot; the din was deafening.

A light flared dimly behind the window and men bulged into the street, peering and swearing. Arms waved, and voices were raised in violent altercation.

"Appears they don't know what happened," giggled Rosalee. "Looks like they're blaming it on somebody at the front door. I wouldn't have given Crane and Wilbur credit for being so smart. They must have heard we were at the Silver Rail together; and when they didn't find us there, they figured we might be at the Quetzal, where they know I go sometimes. Guess they didn't figure on me shooting out the lights."

"I didn't, either," Dixon said grimly.

"I'll wager they hightailed in a hurry after that," Rosalee said with another giggle. "Yes, they were really smart. Had somebody planted at the back door in case we tried to slip out that way. I guess he got a surprise, too."

Dixon's brows knit. "Funny, though, that he'd take a shot at us if he knew you would be with me," he said.

"It does look funny," Rosalee agreed thoughtfully. "Perhaps he lost his temper when you hit him."

"Perhaps," Dixon conceded without conviction,

"but it looks to me like somebody else was mixed up in the business."

"Yes? Who?"

"I haven't the slightest idea," Dixon replied. "But it looks funny."

"You could be right," she agreed. "Perhaps someone was taking advantage of what looked like an opportunity to even up a score. Look! Everybody's going back inside. I think it's safe for us to slip along on this side of the street. Dark over here."

Walking slowly and keeping close to the buildings, where the shadow was deepest, they made their way unmolested back to the centre of town. Rosalee halted in front of the Muerto Hotel.

"I'm going to bed," she announced. "I've had enough excitement for one evening, and I had a hard ride, too. Left Lenton before you did and rode fast to keep in front of you and out of sight. So long!"

"Wait," Dixon protested. "When am I going to see you again?"

"Oh, you'll get a chance sometime—or make one," she replied. "You go back to the Silver Rail now, as if nothing had happened." Before he could protest further, she entered the hotel, smiling at him over her shoulder as the door closed behind her.

Dixon walked warily on his way to the Silver Rail, but nothing untowards happened. He found the boys still whooping it up. Turner and Billy Flint glanced at him expectantly.

"She was tired and went to bed," he answered the unspoken question in their eyes. Turner nodded, but Flint looked speculative.

At that moment, a diversion occurred. One of the

Cross W hands who had been browsing around came back to join the others.

"One of the Bar A boys just told me there was one whale of a row at that Mexican place down at the end of the street," he announced. "Seems some fellers came in the door, shot out the lights and hightailed. He said that right after the lights went out there was shooting in the alley back of the saloon. But when they got the lights on and went to see, they couldn't find anybody. Nobody seemed to know what it was all about."

"Must have been somebody who don't like Mexicans," another hand hazarded.

Billy Flint gave Dixon a strange look. "How'd you skin your knuckles?" he asked.

Dixon glanced down at his right hand and realized that the knuckles were slightly skinned and oozing blood. In the excitement he hadn't noticed it.

"Ran into a door," he said.

"Doors do get in the way sometimes," Flint agreed. His eyes crinkled at the corners, but he did not pursue the subject.

The Silver Rail was lively, but good-naturedly so. Dixon concluded that there was little chance of serious trouble developing. He decided to leave the boys to their own devices and call it a night.

"I'll meet you here around noon and we'll head back to the spread," he told them.

CHAPTER TEN

SHORTLY AFTER THE row in the Quetzal, Crane and Wilbur Roberts entered a saloon at the far end of the street. They spotted Craig Sherwood sitting alone at a table and walked over and joined him. Sherwood glanced at them expectantly.

"Well, did you find them?" he asked.

"No, we didn't," replied Wilbur, who usually did the talking for the pair. "We went to that Mexican place, the Quetzal, where you said they'd be. Maybe they were there; I don't know. Just as we stepped in the door, a fight started, somebody shot out the lights, and the whole joint blew sky high. We went away from there in a hurry."

Sherwood looked apprehensive. "I hope nothing happened to Rosalee, if she was there," he said. Wilbur shrugged his heavy shoulders.

"Rosalee can take care of herself," he replied indifferently. "I wouldn't be surprised if she started the row for some reason or other. Would be just like her."

"Rosalee knows what she's about," said Sherwood. "But I wonder why she allows that devil to keep hanging around her," he added querulously.

Wilbur shrugged again. "Who can figure what a woman does or why she does it," he answered. "Well, we're going to bed. See you tomorrow."

They lumbered out. Sherwood sat on at the table,

watching the doors. He straightened up as they swung open and a big, powerful-looking, thick-shouldered man walked in, glancing about. He spotted Sherwood, crossed the room and slumped into a chair, exhibiting a gorgeous black eye and a swollen jaw.

"What the devil happened to you, Trevis?" Sherwood demanded in astonishment.

"I thought you said that hellion was a paper-back!" Trevis countered wrathfully. "I was never hit so hard in my life; I thought the sky had caved in on me. When I reached for him, he let me have it—one, two! and I was down on my back. I managed to throw some lead at him as he skalleyhooted down the alley."

Sherwood fairly leaped from his chair. "Was the girl with him?" he demanded.

"Reckon she was," Trevis replied. "I forgot all about her."

The Cross W boys arrived at the ranch-house shortly before sundown; the chuck wagon rolled in an hour later and old Estaban proceeded to throw supper together. The tired cowboys went to bed early, but Dixon sat by the window of his room, smoking and thinking.

He was in a restless and irritable mood and not at all in the humour for sleep. Abruptly he rose to his feet, repaired to the stable, got the rig on Rojo and headed south by west. Maybe a long ride would settle his nerves.

It was a beautiful moonless, starry night. A soft hush was over the valley, broken only by the occasional cry of some night bird. Dixon breathed deeply of the crisp air. The unbearable tension lessened. Gradually he was conscious of a growing drowsiness. He turned Rojo's head; he shouldn't have any trouble getting to sleep now.

It was past midnight when he reached the ranch-house yard. Everything appeared quiet and peaceful. Facing him and less than a hundred yards distant was the haymow window of the big barn.

Suddenly the blank window glowed red. Dixon stared in astonishment; then he understood. The mow, crammed with hay, was afire. And there were horses in the barn! He sent Rojo racing towards the building, jerked his right-hand gun and emptied it into the air, shouting at the top of his voice. With the golden horse still in full stride, he leaped from the saddle, reeled, stumbled caught his balance and raced towards the barn door, which stood wide open. The mow was now a raging inferno. The frenzied horses were squealing and snorting.

A man loomed in the open door, the red glow behind him glinting on the gun he held in his hand. Dixon hurled himself sideways an instant before a lance of fire darted towards him. He heard the whine of the passing slug, whipped out his left-hand gun and shot from the hip.

The man in the door reeled back with a cry. Weaving and ducking, Dixon sped forward, reached the door. From the rear of the barn, where the stairs ascended to the mow, gushed orange flame. Dixon's hat turned sideways on his head. He fired again and again. Another cry echoed the shots, and the thud of a falling body, dimly heard above the roar of the burning mow and the screams of the horses.

The cowboys, in all stages of undress, were streaming from the bunkhouse, yelping with alarm.

"The horses!" Dixon roared. "Get the horses out! The mow floor'll fall in at any minute!" He darted into the barn, tore loose a halter and fought to bring a frenzied animal through the heat and smoke to the outside. The hands, cursing and yelling, followed his example. One by one the horses were herded to safety. Sparks were raining down, flames licking through the ceiling boards. The heat was stifling, the air thick with smoke.

Last out was Billy Flint, blood streaming down his face from a gash in his forehead as he battled an insane cayuse that strove to rush into the burning building. Dixon and Bob Turner leaped to help him. Billy stumbled and fell, to lie gasping.

When the horse was at a safe distance, Dixon ran back to Flint and knelt beside him.

"Loco devil hit me in the head with a front foot," the cowboy panted. "I'm all right now. Help me up."

"You lie still until we take care of that head," Dixon told him. "You caught a hard lick."

From the depths of the blazing barn came a scream, a horrible high-pitched shriek of agony and terror.

"Good God!" Dixon exclaimed. "The hellion isn't dead—he's burning up!"

He leaped to his feet and raced for the barn door. Bob Turner howled in amazement:

"Where you going, you crazy fool?"

"Man in there—man I shot," Dixon flung over his shoulder. "Can't leave him to die like that." Turner screeched a protest. Billy Flint strove to rise but fell back groaning. From the barn came scream after scream. Dixon ducked his head and leaped through the door. The heat and smoke struck him like a giant fist. He stumbled to his knees, flung himself flat on his face and began to crawl; there was still a little air along the floor.

By the light of the fiery glow pouring down the blazing stairs, he could dimly make out a writhing body lying at their foot. He floundered forward, sparks and hot brands raining down on him. Above, the burning floor creaked and groaned.

Dixon scrambled to the screaming man, gripped him by the collar, lurched around and crawled frantically towards the door.

Progress was agonizingly slow. His head was spinning. There was no air to breathe; his strength was going. The stairway fell, showering him with stinging sparks. Summoning the last of his ebbing strength, he fought frantically to escape a fiery death. No use! He couldn't make it. The mow floor was sagging. He fell forward, flat on his face, tried to rise and couldn't.

Feet pounded beside him. Hands seized him and his burden and hauled both through the door. Dixon gulped a great draught of life-giving air. Even as his feet cleared the threshold, the mow fell in with a thunderous crash. The roof followed, and the whole building was soon but a shapeless mass spouting smoke and flames in every direction.

The cowboys dragged him to safety and beat out the fire that smouldered in his clothes. Dixon managed to get to his knees and gazed down at the man he had rescued, who was horribly burned about the face and neck. The front of his blood-drenched shirt was streaming. Low moans came from between his seared lips.

"Fellow, why did you do it?" Dixon asked.

"He—he paid me to—" the other gasped.

"He? Who?"

"Him—the big feller—he—he—"

The sobbing breath rattled in the dying man's throat.

His chest arched mightily as he fought for air. It sank, and did not rise again. The glazed eyes gazed fixedly at the star-strewn sky.

Val Dixon got painfully to his feet. His back smarted, his hair was singed, his lashes stuck together. But there was compassion in his eyes as he gazed down at the still form.

"Poor devil paid an awful price for what he did," he said. "How's Billy?"

"I'm okay," said Flint's voice behind him. "What happened?"

Dixon gestured to the dead man. "He must have set the mow afire. I got here just as it blazed up. Met him at the door and we shot it out. He fell at the foot of the stairs and I thought he was dead. He wasn't, and the fire got him."

For a moment there was stunned silence; then: "Ain't there nothing they won't do?"

Dixon could find no words with which to answer him.

"Put the horses in the corral," he said in a tired voice. "And see if you can find the one he rode; it must be around close somewhere."

"Hope it has a Walking R brand on its hide," growled Turner.

"It won't have," Dixon predicted. He looked at the burning barn.

"Lucky there's no wind," he observed. "Otherwise the house might catch too. Guess it's safe enough now."

"Maybe, but I aim to stay up and keep watch till that fire burns down," said Turner. "I'll cover this carcass with a blanket and leave it where it is. Guess we'd better send word to the sheriff about what happened, eh?"

Dixon nodded; he was too tired to argue. "Come along, Billy, and I'll tie your head up," he said. "Hurt much?"

"Aches a little, but it's just a scratch," replied Flint. "And you need some grease on your back and face; you look done to a turn."

"For a little while in there I figured I'd be done to a finish," Dixon said with a faint grin. "If it hadn't been for you fellows charging in there like you did, I'm afraid I'd have been a goner."

"I couldn't make it," said Flint. "Tried to, but I couldn't. Had just got on my feet when they came dragging you out. It was a loco thing for you to do, to go in after that hellion, but it sure showed guts. Come on; let's go to the house. I could stand a mite of coffee right now."

CHAPTER ELEVEN

VAL DIXON DIDN'T know it, but old Clanton Roberts was present at the inquest on the slain firebug, sitting in the back of the room. The patriarch of the Roberts clan rode out of town in a furious temper. That night there was a fiery scene at the Walking R ranch-house.

"Why did you do it?" roared Clanton, shaking his fist under Blount's nose.

"We didn't do it," his son denied. "Do you think we'd take a chance on burning a lot of horses alive just to make trouble for Dixon?"

"Well," snapped Clanton, "everybody in town blames you for doing it."

"Dixon has the idiots hypnotized," declared Blount.

"Dixon didn't accuse you or anybody else," his father answered. "He just told a straight story of how he came to kill that sidewinder they were settin' on."

"Uh-huh, but you don't know what all he said afterwards," sneered Blount. "And I'll tell you something else. Rosalee had dinner with him in Lenton the other night, and again in Muerto."

"Rosalee is free and twenty-one and has a right to have dinner with anybody she's a mind to," retorted Clanton.

"Are you taking up for Dixon?" demanded Blount.

"No, I'm not taking up for him," Clanton replied, "But I'm not banging my head against a stone wall. I'm beginning to think that bucking Dixon was a mistake. Oh, I know I took part in it, in the beginning. but being a fool once doesn't mean you have to keep on being a fool. The way things are working out, we're bucking a lot more than Dixon. I don't stick my head in the sand like a fool ostrich and pretend things ain't so because I don't want to see them. Folks used to do what we told 'em to because they figured it was the best thing to do. Now they're beginning to wonder."

"Get rid of Dixon and things will be like they used to," Blount declared viciously.

"Uh-huh, and get rid of a keg of dynamite and you won't have no explosion," snorted Clanton. "But trying to get rid of it may set one off that'll blow you sky high."

Blount glared at his father, turned and stalked from the room, the twins, Crane and Wilbur, dutifully following their leader.

Outside, Blount relieved his feelings with an explosive oath. "The Old Man's getting dotty," he declared, his scarred face twisting with anger. "From now on I'll handle things by myself."

Materials for the new barn were delivered to the Cross W the following day via freight wagons. The cowboys got busy at once, making foundations for king posts, anchoring beams and setting plates and slips. For the next two weeks Val Dixon was too busy to think much about feuds, wilful ladies or lovers' quarrels. Each night found him thoroughly tired out, the mornings with his hands full of chores and problems.

"She's a good one, better than the old." Bob Turner chuckled through a mouthful of nails as he pounded shingles securely into place. "Cost something, though, didn't it?"

"Yes," Dixon nodded, "but fortunately we have the money to pay for it. Getting that herd through was a lifesaver."

"Somebody else will pay for it, through the nose," Turner declared vindictively. "You watch and see if they don't."

Dixon nodded and did not argue the point. Nothing would convince old Bob that the Robertses weren't responsible for the burning; to try to do so would be a waste of words.

Dixon had not forgotten his resolve to try to learn if stolen cattle were really being driven south through Silver River Canyon. At first he had been inclined to dismiss the matter as a fabrication of the Robertses for the purpose of stirring up trouble and casting suspicion on himself. However, the clearing away of the rock fall which blocked the canyon had changed the complexion of things. That action on the part of somebody predicated usage of the canyon as a route to the south. And nowadays there was practically no legitimate traffic through the dismal gorge. But somebody certainly did not go to the trouble of moving several tons of rock from the trail just for an afternoon's amusement.

He had ordered Turner to keep a constant and careful check on his own stock in the possibility that the Cross W might be losing cows. This, however, had been largely suspended during the building of the barn. But now the new structure was completed, the hands were now busy combing the brakes and draws and getting as accurate as possible. If he was losing cattle, he wanted to know about it and to take steps to put a stop to the pilfering.

If his stock was really being rustled, the procedure

would very likely follow a familiar pattern; nothing spectacular like the running off of a big herd to the accompaniment of lashing quirts and snapping slickers. A few head here, a few head there, quietly and without fanfare. A constant drain on his resources that no owner could withstand for long. The Robertses could evolve no more effective campaign to drive him from the valley—if the Robertses were responsible.

The second night after the completion of the new barn, Dixon slipped quietly from the ranch-house a little after twelve o'clock. He got the rig on Rojo and led the big sorrel some distance from the building before mounting. Then, satisfied that he had aroused none of the sleeping inmates of the bunkhouse, he sent the horse west by slightly south at a good pace. His chore was to find out if cows were being run through the canyon, and he figured he could handle it better by himself. If Turner or Billy Flint knew what he had in mind, he would insist on coming along. And Dixon believed that a single rider would have a better chance to escape detection than would several.

Once again it was a night of stars and no moon; a very silent night, with only the faintest of breeze stirring the grass heads. Dixon knew that sounds would carry a long way in the stillness and was careful to keep Rojo from kicking a loose stone or snapping twigs where the chaparral encroached on the trail.

He passed the point where the trail forked and the old track used by the Indians wound up the slope. It looked shadowy and unreal, a gloomy trough in the growth, devoid of sound or motion. Just the same he studied it carefully as he rode past. It was ridiculous to think that somebody would be up there keeping a watch, but he took no chances and sighed in relief when the tall brush closed in again and he was hidden from possible spying eyes. Another mile and he drew near the black mouth of Silver River Canyon.

Slowing Rojo's pace, he searched out a spot in a nearby thicket where he could lie concealed and see, without being seen, anything that passed along the trail to the canyon.

Tediously the hours passed, with nothing to relieve the great emptiness or break the vast silence. The stars paled from gold to silver, dwindled to needle points of flame piercing the blue-black robe of the sky. A wan glow grew in the east. With a disgusted oath, Dixon mounted and headed home. All was quiet when he reached the ranch-house. He stabled his horse and went to bed for a few hours' sleep.

The second night was a repetition of the first, the third equally barren of results. Once he thought he heard a steer bleat querulously in the distance, but the sound was not repeated and he attributed it to his overwrought imagination.

The third night Dixon suffered the most dreaded accident of the rangeland. He was taking a short cut across the prairie to avoid a wide bend in the trail when Rojo suddenly plunged forward and fell. Dixon, caught wholly unprepared, was hurled from the saddle like a stone from a catapult. He struck the ground with stunning force, a wave of blackness swept over him and he lay without sound or motion. Rojo floundered his front foot from the badger hole that had been his undoing, snorted angrily, limped a few paces and stood gazing inquiringly at his prostrate master.

When he got his senses back, Dixon knew from the

position of the stars that he could have been unconscious but a short time. He struggled to a sitting position, a wave of nausea swept over him, and for a few minutes he sat with his head in his hands, fighting the sickness. Finally it passed and he took stock of himself. He was stiff and sore and there was a lump on the side of his head; but no limb refused to function, there was no joint that would not bend. He cast an apprehensive glance at his horse, got painfully to his feet and examined the front leg of Rojo held slightly raised. With great relief he decided that the limb was not broken; only sprained.

"Figure you can pack me, feller?" he asked, stroking the sorrel's glossy neck. Rojo snorted what was apparently assent. Dixon crawled painfully into the saddle and resumed his interrupted journey, reaching the ranch-house without further mishap.

When Bob Turner rode in to the ranch-house late that afternoon, he had a surprise for Dixon.

"We're losing cows," he said sententiously and without preamble.

"Yes? What makes you think so?" Dixon asked.

"I don't think; I know," Turner replied emphatically. "Last night we lost nigh onto fifty head."

Dixon stared at him incredulously. "Sure you're not imagining things?" he queried.

Old Bob snorted angrily. "Listen," he said, "I know how to tally cows, and I don't make mistakes. I've had my eye on a bunch holed up in the mouth of the canyon over to the south-west for several days. Yesterday they were there, same as usual. This morning they weren't."

Dixon was still incredulous; nothing could have passed through Silver River Canyon last night or the night before without him noticing it. For a moment he was tempted to inform Turner of his fruitless vigil at the canyon mouth, but after an instant's reflection he decided against it. Very likely the missing cows were holed up in some gorge or dry wash the range boss had overlooked. He decided to temporize.

"Check again tomorrow and see what you find," he said.

"Okay," Turner replied, "but I can tell you right now what I'll find—nothing."

"Maybe you're right, but give it a whirl anyhow," Dixon said. Turner grunted and turned to other matters.

Worn out and still stiff and sore from the fall, Dixon resolved to take a night off. Having had very little sleep of late, he went to bed early. The following day he pottered about the house and the yard, catching up with some book work and other chores. The hands were busy filling the new mow with hay. All except Turner and Billy Flint, who were making a careful check of the south-west pastures.

When they returned at sundown, the range boss had not changed his opinion.

"They're gone, and that's all there is to it," he reported.

"There isn't a crack over there we didn't go into," Flint added. "As you know, the canyons are all shallow boxes, and we combed them to the end walls. We're short fifty head, maybe more."

"All right," Dixon said. "Tomorrow we'll try and figure something."

Midnight found him again riding west, mounted on a big dun that had fair speed and endurance, Rojo's leg not yet being fit for travel. Reaching the thicket where he had spent the previous nights, he holed up and waited.

An hour passed and he heard something that snapped every faculty wide awake: the sound of hoofbeats coming from the east, faint with distance but steadily drawing nearer. He crept to the outer fringe of the growth, from where he had a good view of the star-shimmered trail.

Louder and louder sounded the rhythmic pounding. Dixon strained his eyes towards the dark mass of the chaparral. He hadn't long to wait. From the shadows bulged a compact group of horsemen, riding two and two; Dixon counted eight altogether. They swept forward and passed within a few yards of where he crouched amid the growth. Their forms were blurred and indistinct, their faces whitish blobs in the faint starlight. A moment later the black mouth of the canyon swallowed them.

Dixon's palms were sweating. He realized that he had been holding his breath and exhaled sharply. His mind worked at racing speed, trying to evaluate what he had seen, to plan a course of action. Without doubt the group were the marauders he sought. Where were they going? What did they have in mind? The answers to those questions were vital, but how the devil to get them! Should he stay where he was and await the band's possible return? Or should he follow them, a hazardous undertaking, and try to track them to their lair, wherever that was? He wondered why they had not been driving stolen cattle before them, seeing that they were headed south. Perhaps they planned to meet others and return for a raid on the unprotected pastures. What the devil *should* he do! He listened intently, but the beat of hoofs had ceased, which meant they were inside the confining walls of the canyon. He made up his mind to follow. Swinging into the saddle, he sent the dun through the straggle of growth and onto the starlit trail. And at that instant the dun took it into his head to neigh. Dixon grabbed frantically for his nose, an instant too late.

Clear and loud rang the shrill whinny, with a singular carrying quality. The group of riders, no great distance inside the gorge, must have heard it.

The curse Dixon started to fling at the horse died on his lips as from the black opening less than a hundred yards distant came a startled shout. The group had not ridden on through the canyon but had paused in the gloom of its mouth. The dun had unwittingly saved his life.

Another shout. A gun blazed, the report thundering between the rocky walls. A bullet fanned his face. Dixon whirled the dun and sent him charging for the sheltering growth beyond the bend. He bent low in the saddle as more shots sounded and slugs buzzed past him like angry hornets.

Val Dixon was in a bad spot, and he knew it; odds of eight to one were a bit lopsided. And to make matters much worse, he quickly realized that the dun was no match for the mounts of the pursuers. The big horse was giving his all, but it was not enough. Slowly but steadily the pursuit was closing the gap. Dixon had a start of a few hundred yards and believed he could hold it through the stand of chaparral; but the fairly clear prairie beyond would be a different matter. He was within easy rifle range, and the starshine, though faint, was still bright enough to provide fair shooting light. Maybe he could reach some spot where he could hole up and fight it out, but that was doubtful; the canyons and draws which scored the south wall of the valley were still some distance ahead, and the trail veered away from them.

These thoughts and others whirled through Dixon's mind as he urged the dun to greater speed. Something had to be done, and there was little time in which to do it.

Directly ahead was the point where the trail forked. He reached it and swerved the dun sharply to the right, onto the old track that wound up the south slope. Maybe the pursuers would be fooled by the manoeuvre and charge ahead on the main trail.

That hope was short-lived. A chorus of shouts sounded, then the steady pounding of hoofs to his rear.

The crooked trail up the slope might provide an opportunity for a desperate man. A sharp bend or a clump of rock might give him a chance to make a stand. Besides, the dun, while lacking speed, was a powerful animal and might be able to hold his own on the steep and rugged slope, if he could just make it in time.

They reached the slope and breasted it. And now Dixon knew his life hung in the balance. He braced himself for the feel of a bullet tearing through his body. He held his breath, tensed his muscles. The faint starlight suddenly was like the blaze of noon, the infrequent stands of brush which flanked the track miles apart. Surely they must be able to see him !

But no shot rang out to tumble the echoes far and wide. No sound broke the stillness save the clatter of pursuing hoofs, threading through the clash and thud of his own mount's irons on the rocky trail. Dixon expelled his breath and relaxed a little. Directly ahead the chaparral closed in and the track wound through deepest gloom. His keen hearing told him the dun was holding his own, although now he was labouring, his breath coming in moaning sobs, his coat drenched with sweat.

"Those broncs back there must be in the same shape, though, feller," he comforted the horse. "Hard going for them, too."

The dun essayed a weak snort of dubious agreement and floundered on. Dixon strained his eyes in an endeavour to probe the gloom ahead. Suddenly he uttered an exultant exclamation. The growth had thinned for some two score yards, and beyond the clearing loomed a clump of chimney rocks.

"This is it, horse," he said, "the best chance we'll ever have." He swerved the animal around the rocks and swung to the ground, sliding his Winchester from the saddle boot. Crouched behind a jut of stone, he rested the rifle barrel upon it and drew a bead on the black opening where the bristle of thick brush encroached on the trail.

Into view stormed the pursuers, a dark block of movement, their horses foaming. Dixon squeezed the trigger.

A wailing curse echoed the report, and just as he fired a second time, a horse reared high. "Darn!" he muttered as the poor beast went down, kicking furiously in its death agonies and hurling its rider into the brush.

Nevertheless, the unfortunate animal served a good purpose; its body blocked the trail. A second horse fell over it. For the moment the pursuit was in utter confusion.

Dixon fired again and again. Flame gushed towards him and answering shots spattered the boulder or clipped the leaves overhead. But a man on a plunging horse is not in a good shooting stance, and he was in the deeper shadow. Another yell sounded as a bullet went home. Then the group whirled their frantic mounts and went streaking back the way they had come, a man on foot scuttling after them. Dixon lined sights with his back, then changed his mind and lowered the rifle. No use to kill somebody if he didn't have to. He listened intently, but the clattering hoof beats told him they were still going. He ran to where his own cayuse stood with heaving sides, mounted and rode on at the fastest pace the exhausted dun could manage. Leaning over, he patted the horse's neck.

"If it hadn't been for you taking a notion to sing a song to the stars, I'd have barged smack into those hellions there in the canyon mouth and gotten blown from under my hat," he told the dun. "Thanks, feller; you're okay."

A little later the trail forked, an even narrower track slanting more to the east. Dixon took it. It might serve to confuse the devils if they decided to come on once they had mastered their demoralized mounts. A mile or so farther on he came to another fork. He turned into the one that ran almost due east. It also branched, and branched again. The hills were a maze of tracks, speckled with clumps of growth. Doubtless they had been made by the Indians who once roamed the uplands. Soon he was utterly confused and hadn't the slightest idea where he was or how to escape from the bewildering labyrinth.

"But we 'pear to be heading east all the time," he told the horse. "Come daylight, maybe we can get our bearings. Listen! Don't I hear water somewhere ahead? Yes, I do, and we can both sure stand a drink. June along, feller; I think we can risk holding up for a short spell to give you a chance to catch your breath."

A few minutes later the starshine glinted on the surface of a shallow brook that foamed across the track to tumble down a steep slope. Grass grew on its banks, so Dixon flipped the bit from the dun's mouth and loosened the cinches. After both had drunk their fill, the horse began contentedly cropping. Dixon stretched out on the ground, rolled a cigarette and relaxed in comfort.

Overhead the stars were paling and the smell of dawn was in the air. Fairly confident that he had shaken off the pursuit, he resolved to wait until daylight before moving on. No sense in groping his way through the dark; he'd just become more confused. He rolled another cigarette, listened to the music of the brook and watched the stars dwindle and go out.

The sky brightened swiftly. Birds began singing in the thickets. The solid blocks of shadow developed fuzzy edges, greyed, faded into nothingness. Dixon stood up, yawned and stretched. Nearby the dun had finished feeding and stood regarding him contemplatively. He tightened the cinches, replaced the bit and mounted.

It was mid-morning when, after following a maze of old tracks that apparently began nowhere and ended in the same place, he reached a point, far to the east, where he could view the prairie below. There followed another long and tortuous ride down the slope. He breathed deep relief when he reached level ground again. Around noon he arrived home, hot, tired and ravenously hungry.

CHAPTER TWELVE

WHEN TURNER AND Flint arrived at the ranch-house the following day, they bore news.

"Those darned Roberts twins, Crane and Wilbur, were in town last night," Turner announced. "Nope, we didn't run into them, but we talked with a feller who did. He said they told him they'd been losing cows again and that night before last they rode down to that blasted canyon with a bunch of their hands, aiming to try and get a line on the thieves. Said they spotted one, all right, and tried to run him down, but lost him in the hills."

Turner paused to light a cigarette, then resumed with a chuckle :

"Feller was a salty hombre, all right. One of the hands got a hole through his arm, another had a hunk of meat knocked off his leg, and another one lost his horse. Seems the feller holed up behind some rocks and mowed 'em down. They said their cayuses went plumb loco and bolted, and before they could get 'em under control the jigger was gone in the hills. If you ask me, I'd say it was *them* who hightailed. They said the hands who were hurt needed attention, so they called it a night and went back to their *casa*. What do you think of that yarn, Val ?"

"Sounds interesting," Dixon replied in non-committal tones. "I've a notion they were telling the truth."

"Must have strained them a mite if they were," grunted Turner. "I'd say it would be a sorta novel experience for those hellions to tell something that was so."

Dixon nodded and did not pursue the conversation. He wanted to think and plan a course of action.

So, unbeknownst, he had tangled with the Robertses. Such a diagnosis was fantastic, but it was reasonable to assume that the boys would agree with Turner.

For long moments he sat staring straight ahead of him. Then he got to his feet and walked out into the sunshine to gaze west by south towards the distant hills.

The dark hour before the dawn found Val Dixon riding west along the trail that led to Silver River Canyon. He rode warily, although he had little fear that anybody would be abroad at that time of night. If the Robertses had posted a guard on the canyon mouth during the hours of darkness, they would not use the trail to return to their ranch-house, far to the northeast, but would diagonal across the prairie. And possible wide-loopers would most assuredly not use it; of that he was convinced.

It was daylight when he reached the forks. He halted Rojo and sat gazing at the crooked track winding up the slope, clearly visible for several hundred yards, then vanishing in the bristle of growth. He rolled a cigarette and smoked slowly, still gazing at the trail. After a bit he pinched out the butt, gathered up the split reins and turned Rojo's head to the left. Soon he reached the slope and began the winding climb, his eyes studying the trail ahead.

"Steep," he muttered, "but not too steep. Yes, cows could make it up here without any trouble."

Very quickly he spotted indubitable evidence that

cattle had passed that way a short time before. Of course it could have been some mavericking mossy-backs hunting fresh pastures, as old critters sometimes did, but Dixon did not think so. Well, he'd soon find out. After a while the trail levelled off, following a bench that curved around the hills some distance below their crest. It was undoubtedly very old and probably narrower than it once had been, but still broad enough for three horsemen to ride abreast, or an equal number of cattle.

The trail through Silver River Canyon was different. Although not a frequented thoroughfare, it was used occasionally by single horsemen or groups riding up from the south. For the cow thieves to drive their purloined stock through the canyon was to invite detection.

Why had nobody thought of the old trail as the outlaw route? Dixon wondered about that for a while; the answer was comparatively simple. In the old days wide-loopers had run cows through the canyon, so everybody concentrated on the canyon when stealing began anew. And so far as he knew, the Walking R had been the only outfit to lose stock until the Cross W also began suffering. The Robertses had jumped to the conclusion that the Cross W was responsible, and had reasoned that the canyon opening onto Cross W land would be their logical route.

But why had the hellions gone to the trouble of clearing the rock fall from the canyon trail? That one puzzled him for a while until abruptly he swore at his own denseness. To strengthen the belief that the canyon trail was the route used, of course.

All in all, Val Dixon was beginning to feel quite proud of himself. As a range detective he wasn't doing so badly. He had solved the mystery of Star Drive

Valley, and the thieves sliding up from the wild country to the south were in for an unpleasant surprise. He rode on, taking careful note of his surroundings.

Finally he reached the southern terminus of the hills. The trail slithered down a fairly gentle slope to reach the level ground below and dim away into the distance. A couple of miles to the east, Silver River flowed from the canyon likewise to vanish into the rugged fastnesses of the lower Big Bend.

For a long time he sat gazing across the wild and lonely but weirdly beautiful vista; then he turned his horse and rode back the way he had come, arriving at the ranch-house late in the afternoon.

That night he called the hands into the living-room and regaled them with an account of the week's hectic happenings and what he had learned. Astonished oaths and ejaculations greeted the story.

"But I still figure we'll find the Robertses somewhere at the bottom of the heap," stubborn old Bob Turner declared. "What we going to do? Hole up down there and blow 'em from under their hats?"

"Yes, we'll do that, but in a law-abiding manner," Dixon replied. "Tomorrow I'm riding to town for a talk with the sheriff."

Sheriff Floyd Jarrett's astonishment was on a par with that of the Cross E cowboys when Dixon sat in his office and talked the following afternoon. He shook his head, pulled his moustache and rumbled profanity.

"Son, you may have hit on something," he said when Dixon paused. "Yes, you may have. I'll be frank with you. I believed the Robertses were lying when they claimed they were losing cows, but it begins to look like maybe they weren't. It's just possible that the outlaws operating to the east and south of here might be responsible, although that don't seem likely. The Texas Rangers are on the trail of those horned toads, and it don't 'pear exactly reasonable to think they'd slide way up here just to wide-loop some cows. Cattle stealing is more vulnerable than other kinds of thieving; you can't hide a herd of cows in a saddle pouch. So they'd be laying themselves open, without a great deal of gain.

"That is," he added thoughtfully, "unless they had some reason for wanting the feud between you and the Robertses to keep b'ilin'."

"I hadn't thought of that," Dixon said. "Why would anybody want the feud to keep on?"

"Hard to tell," replied the sheriff. "Somebody might have hatched a scheme to grab onto a valuable property, such as that end of Star Drive Valley represents. Say for instance you and the Robertses succeeded in crippling each other some way—sort of far-fetched to think of, but it could work out like that—and you both had to get out or sell out. Somebody might be all set to profit. Such things have been done, you know; happened like that over in New Mexico."

"And that would most likely mean a local person or a local outfit would be mixed up in it," observed Dixon.

"So I'd presume," agreed the sheriff. "All this is sort of loco thinking, though. More likely to be some brush-poppin' bunch grabbin' off a few crooked pesos. But if a bunch sliding up from the south are responsible and we can drop a loop on them, it may help to bring the Robertses to their senses before something really bad happens."

"That's the way I feel about it. I hope it will work out," said Dixon. "Don't you think where the trail forks is the spot to set a trap?"

The sheriff nodded. "Looks that way to me," he conceded. "Tell you what: we'll make a try at it tomorrow night. I've got to go to Carlos in the morning —another bank robbery over there—but I'll get back in time to make it down to the forks around midnight. I've a notion it would be a good idea for you and your boys to drop down there a bit earlier, say about ten o'clock, just in case. I'll swear you in as a special sheriff and you can take your boys along as a posse. I don't think anything is liable to break until the dark hours just before morning, but we won't take any chances. Okay?" Dixon nodded.

The sheriff accompanied Dixon to the door. On the steps they paused for a last word.

"Then it's all set?" Dixon said.

"Yes," replied Jarrett. "I'll meet you down there tomorrow night."

A man who was passing glanced sharply at them, hesitated and walked on. Engrossed in their conversation, neither Dixon nor the sheriff noticed him.

That night, the Roberts family and Craig Sherwood, who had ridden down for a visit, were assembled in the living-room when Cliff White, the Walking R range boss, burst in, his eyes glowing with excitement.

"Say," he exclaimed without preamble, "I think something's in the wind. I was passing by the sheriff's office this afternoon, and Jarrett and Val Dixon came out together. I heard Jarrett say something that sounded funny to me."

"What did he say?"

He said, "I'll meet you down there tomorrow night." Now what the devil do you suppose he meant by that? What are those two up to?"

There was a moment of silence; then Blount said:
"Chances are whatever it is, it'll be something we
won't like. Maybe Dixon has hypnotized old Floyd into
helping him with his cow stealing."

Rosalee's lips tightened, but she said nothing. Craig
Sherwood shook his head

"As I've told you before, Blount, I believe you're
barking up the wrong tree," he said. "If you're losing
cows, it's a bunch working up from the south that's
responsible. Mark what I tell you. If you'd pay less
attention to Dixon and more to that canyon down there,
you might get a chance to knock them off. In fact, I
think it would be good sense to lay off Dixon altogether.
He's a cold proposition, and you may not have much
luck tangling with him. You had a little dose of that a
while back."

Blount's choleric face turned red at the intimation
that Val Dixon might be too much for him to handle.
However, his only answer was a grunt.

A little later, Sherwood looked at his watch and rose
to his feet. "Got to be going," he announced. "Busy
day ahead of me tomorrow. I'll be seeing you." His
gaze lingered on Rosalee's face a moment; then he
turned and walked out.

Old Clanton recalled the subject of Dixon and the
sheriff. "What *has* that pair got up their sleeves?" he
demanded querulously of nobody in particular. "Could
be something to do with that blasted barn. Maybe the
hellion Dixon plugged talked some before he cashed in."

Blount shot his father an angry glance. "Who cares!"
he said. "I'm going over to the bunkhouse." He rose
and left the room. Rosalee watched him go, her eyes
thoughtful.

CHAPTER THIRTEEN

UNDER COVER OF darkness the following night, the Cross W outfit rode west, leaving the ranch-house a little after nine o'clock.

"A moon tonight," Dixon observed, glancing at the silver sickle hanging in the western sky. "Not much of a one, but enough to give shooting light before it sets, around one in the morning."

"And light enough to show somebody riding the trail," Billy Flint added significantly.

As they rode, the cowboys except Billy Flint laughed and joked in low tones. He rode in silence, Dixon noted, his eyes constantly scanning his surroundings, probing the trail ahead, roving over groves and thickets.

His evident uneasiness communicated itself to Dixon. He, too, fell silent and grew watchful and alert.

Gradually they neared the point where the trail forked. Billy Flint spoke for the first time in an hour.

"That owl down there is doing a lot of yelling," he said. "Something's got him bothered. Wonder what it is?"

"Coyote, or a snake on a limb, the chances are," guessed Turner.

"Could be," admitted Flint, "but I doubt it."

"What else could it be?"

"I don't know," the cowboy replied, "but something's got him real mad. Listen to him whine!"

"Might be a good notion to stop talking from now on," suggested Dixon. "And slow down."

Silence fell, broken only by the angry screeches of the owl, now no great distance ahead. The cowboys curbed their mounts to a walk. They were almost to the forks.

It was Dixon's alertness and keen hearing that saved them. He heard the muffled snap in the wall of growth, as if somebody had inadvertently trod on a dry stick. "Unfork! Hug the ground!" he shouted.

Even as the cowboys unquestioningly obeyed, flame gushed from the chaparral; the air quivered to a bellow of shots.

One of the hands gave a yelp of pain. Another cursed viciously. A horse screamed its death agony and fell. Flat on the ground, Dixon jerked his guns and emptied them into the growth. The others followed suit. Answering flashes spurted from the brush, accompanied by yells and curses. The din was hellish.

Abruptly Dixon realized that no more were coming from the chaparral.

"Hold it!" he shouted. "Hold it!"

The firing ceased. When their ears had stopped ringing, they heard the sound of fast hoofs fading into the distance.

"After 'em!" yelled Turner, leaping to his feet.

"Wait!" Dixon said. "Get your rifles ready and watch that slope up there. They'll show if they're following the trail."

The others obeyed. Tense and ready, they waited. The minutes dragged past, and the trail up the slope lay silent and deserted.

"Seems they ought to be showing by now," remarked Turner.

"Yes, they should be," answered Dixon. "Wait another minute."

"I guessed wrong," he added a moment later. "They must have headed for the canyon. Come on; maybe we can catch them up. Is anybody bad hurt?"

"Jim and Harley got nicked; nothing serious," replied Turner. "I'll tie 'em up. Ralph lost his horse."

"He'll have to hole up here and wait for us," Dixon said, swinging into the saddle. "All right, let's go. We'll —what the devil?"

From somewhere in the darkness to the south-west came a stutter of shots. For some moments the fusillade continued, then levelled off to several spaced reports.

"What the devil is going on over there?" wondered Turner.

"I don't know, but one thing is sure; we're not riding into it till we know more," Dixon replied.

"Sounds quiet enough now," Flint remarked.

"Yes, but we'll wait and see if it busts loose again," Dixon said. "Those last shots sounded like somebody hightailing with lead following them."

For some minutes the group sat their horses, peering and listening; however, the firing did not resume. Dixon was about to give the word for a cautious advance when one of the hands let out a yelp:

"Look over there!"

Following his pointing finger, Dixon saw, about a mile distant across the prairie and dimly outlined in the dying moonlight, four horsemen speeding east.

"The Robertses!" exploded Turner. "What'd I tell you!"

"Maybe. But what were they shooting at—themselves?" Dixon replied.

"Whoever they are, I think they ran into the bunch that tried to do for us. They were outnumbered and hightailed."

"Hope there were others besides the ones that got away," Turner said vindictively.

"Somebody coming down the trail, coming fast," Billy Flint exclaimed. "Sounds like just one horse."

"Must be the sheriff," said Dixon. "He was supposed to meet us here about now."

"Sheriff or no sheriff, I'm not taking any chances," growled old Bob, unlimbering his rifle. "Watch those other hellions out of sight, you fellers. See they don't circle around behind us."

Soon the rider from the east came bulging into view; it was the sheriff. He pulled his horse to a foaming halt.

"What was all the shooting about?" he demanded.

Dixon told him. Jarrett swore sulphurously. "So they were all set to drygulch you, eh? But how the devil did they know you were headed for here?"

"That's something I'd like the answer to," Dixon returned grimly. "You didn't tell anybody in town what we had in mind, did you?"

The sheriff swore some more. "You know I didn't," he declared indignantly. "Do you think you got any of 'em?"

"I don't know, but I doubt it," Dixon replied. "It was blind shooting. We haven't looked in the brush yet."

"Guess we'd better," decided the sheriff. "If you did get one we might learn something. Reckon its safe to make a light."

Breaking off several sotol stalks for torches, they gave the growth a careful once-over but discovered no bodies.

"Here are some blood spots, though, quite a few of them," Dixon announced. "Looks like some of them got nicked. Nothing serious, the chances are."

Beating out the torches they returned to the trail. "Now what?" Dixon asked.

Sheriff Jarrett tugged his moustache. "Supposing we amble down to that blasted canyon, slow like, and see if we can learn anything there," he suggested. "That shooting down there looks like maybe two bunches got together."

"Maybe the Robertses had a falling out among themselves," Bob Turner observed caustically.

The sheriff didn't waste time arguing the point. "Let's go," he said.

Leaving Ralph Boyd, the horseless puncher, to await their return, they set out, approaching the black canyon mouth with great caution, for now the moon had set and the darkness between the walls was stygian.

No sound came from the gorge, save the moan and mutter of Silver River chafing its rocky banks, but to Val Dixon it gave the eerie impression of a monstrous predatory beast waiting to engulf its prey. He cursed his over-active imagination, but the feeling persisted to such an extent that every nerve was strained to the breaking point. He slipped to the ground.

"I'm going to find out if they're in there," he told the sheriff. Before the old peace officer could protest, he was gliding along in the shadow of the wall. He reached the canyon mouth, hesitated a moment, then sidled into the opening.

Dixon knew he was doing a foolhardy thing. If the marauders actually were holed up in the gorge and discovered him, he'd get short shrift. On the other hand, if they were there, it would be practically impossible for the posse to ride in without being spotted, with all the advantage then on the side of the outlaws; so he felt the risk he took was justified.

Step by step he stole along, hugging the rock wall, pausing often to peer and listen. Already he was several hundred yards inside the canyon and had seen and heard nothing. It began to look as if the hellions, who-ever they were, had kept going.

The moon had set and the stars were bright overhead. Gradually his eyes became accustomed to the faint light they cast into the gorge. He could dimly make out the wall beside him and the rock floor at his feet for a few yards ahead. His caution redoubled, for if he could see, he would also be seen, although he felt pretty sure he'd be able to spot a bunch of horsemen before they per-ceived him.

Abruptly his ears, attuned to the silence broken only by the murmuring water, caught the faintest sounds ahead. He sensed rather than saw movement on the canyon floor, caught a gleam of shifted metal. He was going down and sideways along the wall when a gun spurted fire from the surface of the trail. The report rang out like thunder in the confined space. A slug smacked the wall a few inches from his head. He jerked his own gun and fired at the flash, again and again.

A cry of pain and a clang of metal on the rocks echoed the shots, followed by a gurgling moan, then silence.

Tingling in every nerve, sweat streaming down his face, Dixon crouched against the wall, his gun ready for instant action. He could just make out a dark blob on the trail a few yards ahead; as the minutes passed it did not move. The moan and mutter of the river sounded loud in the continued stillness.

Cautiously he crept towards what was undoubtedly a body, his gun clubbed to strike. Still no sound, no movement. He reached the body and stretched out his free hand. It touched a shirt sticky with congealed blood, then a face which did not move a muscle. Undoubtedly it was a dead man lying at his feet. He surged erect with a gasp as hoofs thundered on the trail behind and voices shouted; then he realized it was the posse coming to find out what was going on. He raised his voice in reassurance.

"Take it easy; don't run over me," he called. "Take it easy; everything's okay."

An instant later the horsemen loomed huge and distorted in the gloom, jerking their horses to a clattering halt.

"What's going on?" bawled the sheriff's voice.

"A jigger lying on the ground tried to down me," Dixon replied. "I think he's dead now."

"He'd better be!" snorted the sheriff as he swung from the saddle. "What a night!"

He fumbled a match from his pocket, struck it and held it low. The tiny flicker revealed a squat form with a mottled face lying prone on the rock floor.

"Dead, all right," said the sheriff as the match flickered out. "Hightail back and find some sotol stalks or dry branches to make a light," he called to the others. "You say the sidewinder threw lead at you, Val? What the devil was he doing layin' there, anyhow?"

"I've a notion he was the one who stopped lead up there by the forks," Dixon replied. "Guess he got weak from loss of blood and toppled off his horse, and the rest either didn't miss him or rode on and left him. His shirt's all sticky with blood, but it isn't fresh blood. I think I knocked his gun from his hand with a slug. We'll see when we get a light."

The sheriff peered into the darkness ahead. "No signs of the rest of 'em coming back," he growled. "Chances are they won't, but keep your eyes skinned, boys."

The hands who had ridden in search of something for torches returned with some sotol stalks. The sheriff lit one which burned briskly, casting light over the scene.

The dead man was a squat, ungainly-appearing individual with a blotched face and reddish hair. His thin lips were open to reveal tobacco-stained teeth. Altogether he was not a very savoury-appearing specimen.

"Uh-huh, got one through the belly," said the sheriff, after a brief examination. "Vicious as a broken-back rattler; used his last breath to try and take somebody with him when he took the Big Jump. You hit his hand all right, Val; fresh blood on it. And there's his iron layin' over there by the wall. Good shootin'!"

"Good luck, you mean," replied Dixon, squatting beside the sheriff. "I just shot blind."

Jim Carstairs, one of the hands peering over Dixon's shoulder, let out an exclamation.

"Say, I've seen this hellion before," he announced. "Darned if I can remember where, but I've seen him; I'll bet on it. I remember that spotted face. Now where in blazes!"

"At a bar, the chances are," said the sheriff. "Try and remember where and who was with him; might mean a good deal."

Carstairs wrinkled his brows and puckered his eyes but shook his head.

"Maybe it'll come to me after a while," he said.

Sheriff Jarrett was going through the dead man's pockets, turning out various odds and ends of no significance and considerable money.

"He was doing all right by himself," he snorted. "He never saved up that much following a cow's tail. Hello, what's this?"

From an inner pocket he took a crumpled envelope. It bore no address but was sealed. The sheriff ripped it open and drew forth a folded sheet of paper. He unfolded it, and he and Dixon peered close at a few lines of writing, which read:

> "Had to buy them from him. He's carrying
> the money. He's leaving town tonight."

"Something to do with his stealing, the chances are," the sheriff remarked disinterestedly, passing the paper to Dixon, who read it again, his brows drawing together, a puzzled expression on his face.

Abruptly his eyes glowed. Glancing at the sheriff, he saw the peace officer was still busy going through the dead man's clothes. He slipped the sheet into his own pocket.

"What shall we do with the carcase?" he asked casually.

"Leave it where it is," decided the sheriff. "Tomorrow, after I've had some sleep, I'll ride down with a spare horse and pack it to town for folks to look over. Somebody might recognize the varmint. We'll have one cayuse packing double tonight, and that's enough. Well, guess we might as well mosey home. Those other sidewinders won't be heading back this way tonight, and they've got too much of a start to be any chance of catching up."

As they mounted, Dixon made another remark or two to hold the sheriff's attention and if possible prevent him from recalling the unsigned scrawl that he, Dixon, had stowed in his pocket. For what had appeared to be of no importance to the sheriff was highly significant to him. He wanted a chance to study it further and decide to just what use it might be put.

On the way back they picked up Ralph Boyd and mounted him behind Dixon, Rojo not objecting to carrying double so long as his master sanctioned it.

Day had broken before they reached the ranch-house. Sheriff Jarrett and the hands immediately tumbled into bed. Dixon, however, tired though he was, did not at once seek his rest. Instead, he spread the crumpled sheet of paper on a table and studied its cryptic message:

"Had to buy them from him. He's carrying the money. He's leaving town tonight."

Very quickly his keen eyesight told him that a word had been carefully erased after the message was written and the word "tonight" substituted. He wondered what the devil the original word could have been. Possibly "tomorrow," he finally concluded.

Although it was unsigned, there was no doubt in Dixon's mind as to who had written the message. None other than Nate Billings, the Lenton cattle buyer. "Them" indubitably meant his cows, which Billings had at first refused to purchase, only to change his mind and become very eager to buy. And the money referred to was that which he had carried in the belt around his waist. Without doubt the message had been meant to inform somebody of that fact.

But who was the mysterious somebody? Dixon hadn't the slightest idea, but he resolved to find out. Already he was evolving a plan of action. Unless his estimate of Billings' character was altogether wrong, he believed it wouldn't be hard to scare the buyer into telling.

One thing he felt was obvious: the message had never reached the person for whom it was intended. For some reason, the mottle-faced outlaw had failed to deliver it and had kept it on his person.

Weary from wrestling with the problem, Dixon went to bed and slept soundly. He was smoking a cigarette after a late breakfast when Jim Carstairs sauntered in.

"Got something to tell you, Boss," the cowboy said, after glancing around to make sure nobody was within hearing distance. "You know that speckle-faced jigger I said I was sure I'd seen somewhere before? Well, all of a sudden it came to me. Boss, that hellion was one of Craig Sherwood's hands. I remember now I saw him with some of the others on Sherwood's south pasture, combing for strays."

Dixon stared at the cowboy. "Jim, are you sure?" he asked.

"Yep, I'm sure," Carstairs answered. "Couldn't make a mistake with a map like that. Feller I saw had the same build, too. What do you make of it?"

"I don't know," Dixon replied. "But Sherwood is always hiring scrubby specimens. You know he can't hold good hands because he's always behind with his wages; he has to hire what he can get and doesn't turn down anything much that comes along." Carstairs nodded his understanding.

"Always seems to have plenty of money for women and cards and whisky," he remarked. "Guess that's why he can't pay his hands."

For several minutes Dixon was silent, turning the matter over in his mind; abruptly he arrived at a conclusion.

"Jim," he said, "I think it would be a good thing to keep this to ourselves, for a while at least. If we spill it, all sorts of loco stories may get started. The sheriff's going to pack the body to town, and the chances are somebody else will spot the fellow as having worked for Sherwood. I think it would be a good idea for us to keep out of it and not be the first to identify him."

"That's what I thought," agreed Carstairs. "That's why I came to you without saying anything to anybody else. Pity I didn't spot the hellion as working for the Robertses."

"That would put a somewhat different complexion on the business," Dixon said. "Okay, we'll keep a tight latigo on our jaws for the present. Has the sheriff ridden to the canyon yet?"

"Left a couple of hours ago," Boyd replied. "Said he wanted to make it to town by dark if he could. He figures to stop here on his way back."

The sheriff did stop at the ranch-house when he arrived late in the afternoon, leading a spare horse that bore no burden. Plainly he was in an uproariously bad temper.

"Why didn't I bring him with me?" he yelped in answer to somebody's question. "Because he wasn't there to bring along, that's why!"

"What do you mean?" sputtered Bob Turner.

"Can't you understand plain English?" snorted the

sheriff. "I said he wasn't there. Somebody had packed him off."

"And what does that mean?" persisted the bewildered Turner.

"It means somebody was mighty anxious to make sure he wouldn't be put on exhibition in town," the sheriff replied grimly.

"Scared he'd be recognized, eh?"

"Yes, and that maybe somebody would remember who he hung out with."

Dixon and Jim Carstairs exchanged glances. Dixon shook his head slightly; Carstairs nodded his understanding. "Come on in, Jarrett, and eat," Dixon invited. "You need to take it easy for a while."

The sheriff grunted assent and entered the ranchhouse. Dixon ordered the horses cared for and followed.

While the sheriff ate, Dixon sat and smoked and tried to think.

Jarrett sucked a final cup of coffee through his moustache and stood up.

"Much obliged for the snack," he said. "I'm heading for town; been away from the office too long already. Drop in on me in a day or two and we'll see what we can figure."

Dixon promised to do so and the sheriff departed. Dixon was left alone with his thoughts. After a considerable period of painful cogitation, he called in Turner and Billy Flint, showed them the letter and confided his suspicions about Nate Billings. Turner and Flint at once agreed it was self-evident that Billings was the author.

"Tomorrow we ride to Lenton and have a little talk with *Señor* Billings," Dixon concluded. "Maybe we can get to the bottom of this mystery."

CHAPTER FOURTEEN

NATE BILLINGS WAS at his desk late the following evening when the three cattlemen walked into his office and closed the door.

"What can I do for you, gentlemen?" he said, looking apprehensive.

Dixon laid the letter on the desk before him. "Billings," he said, without preamble, "I think this requires a bit of explaining."

The buyer stared at the paper with dilated eyes; sweat popped out on his fat face.

"Where did you get this?" he quavered.

Dixon decided to try a shot in the dark. "Billings," he said, "because of that letter you wrote, three men died. Did it ever occur to you that the man to whom you sent it might feel a rope tightening around his neck and try to wriggle out of the loop?"

Nate Billings went to pieces. "I didn't tell Blount Roberts to do anything," he cried. "I just told him I had to buy your infernal cows."

"And just *mentioned* I was packing the money you paid?" Dixon suggested sarcastically.

"I had to tell him I paid you for them," Billings answered, his eyes wild. "I didn't tell him to try and rob you."

"Of course not," Dixon said, again sarcastic. "Just

told him when I would leave town—packing the money."

"I just thought he ought to know when you'd be back in Muerto," Billings mumbled, wetting his dry lips with his tongue.

"I see," said Dixon; "real nice of you. Billings, why did you buy those cows after first refusing to do so? Better come clean, Billings; time *might* be short."

"Very short," added Bob Turner, glowering at the buyer and fingering his holster.

Billings jumped in his chair; his face was streaming sweat now.

"Because Rosalee told me I had to," he answered sullenly. "She was going to wire the office at Kansas City."

Dixon's eyes glowed. Turner and Flint exchanged satisfied glances.

"And Blount had told you not to buy them, eh?"

"That's right," admitted Billings. "He told me to go ahead and buy Sherwood's but not to buy yours."

Flint and Turner again exchanged glances, and this time the young cowboy's eyes were speculative. Dixon was silent for a moment; then:

"Billings, by whom did you send that letter to Blount Roberts?"

"By one of the fellers who got killed when they tried to hold you up—Jess Willoughby."

Dixon's eyes narrowed a trifle but he dissembled his surprise.

"You sure about that?" he asked.

"Yes, I'm sure," replied Billings. "I gave the letter to Jess and told him to get it to Blount. Guess Blount told him what to do," he added meaningly.

"Maybe," Dixon conceded. "And so Blount ordered you not to buy my cows."

"Yes, he did," said Billings. "I had to string along with him. The Robertses run things in this section, and when Blount tells you to do something, you do it, or else."

"You didn't do it that time," Dixon pointed out.

"No," Billings answered, his voice a snarl. "Rosalee is worse than Blount—she's got more brains. She said she'd shoot me if I didn't."

"You had a shooting coming," said Billy Flint, speaking for the first time. "I'm glad she didn't, though. Glad she left that to somebody who'll enjoy it more."

Billings gasped like a rooster with the pip. He shivered, and shrank from the cowboy's icy eyes. Dixon bit back a grin with difficulty.

"Guess that's all for now, Billings," he said. "We'll be seeing you." He turned towards the door.

Billy Flint lingered, his eyes never leaving Billings' contorted face.

"Why not kill him now, Val, instead of later?" he suggested, toying with the butt of his gun. Billings let out a despairing howl.

This time Dixon had even more trouble suppressing a grin, although he suspected that Billy was in deadly earnest. He shook his head.

"Now now," he vetoed the cowboy's suggestion. "We may need him a while longer. Let's go!"

Billy Flint did grin as he turned slowly to the door. Nate Billings seemed to shrivel like an over-ripe peach in the sun.

Outside, old Bob guffawed softly. "Well, we scared the pants off that horned toad," he chortled. "Didn't I tell you the Robertses were mixed up in the business?"

"Yes, the Robertses *were* mixed up in the business, very much so," Dixon replied. "But we didn't learn a great deal beyond what we already knew or suspected. Evidently the fellow Jess handed the letter to, that jigger who died down in the canyon, was told to get it to Blount. Somehow he never got it to Blount, and for some reason kept it instead of tearing it up. Which isn't particularly important, I'd say. What *is* important is the fact that Blount never received the letter. Jess just decided to stage a holdup on his own. That's the way I look at it."

"And you can just bet that the only reason Blount Roberts wasn't in on it was because he didn't get the letter," Turner declared.

"And Rosalee scared Billings into buying your cows," Billy Flint broke in. "Val, that's a gal in a million!"

Dixon was willing to agree, but he only nodded.

"Let's go get a drink," he said.

They repaired to the Widow Maker and had several. Flint and Turner were cheerful and animated, but Dixon was silent. He morosely downed his drink and ordered another round. After that he decided something to eat was in order. He found a vacant table and sat down; Turner and Flint remained at the bar. While he was waiting for his wants to be supplied, old Swayback Sawyer, the owner, lumbered across the room and eased his bulk into the opposite chair. Swayback had taken a liking to Val Dixon, and Swayback's likes and dislikes were strong.

"Well," he said, "still fighting the Robertses?"

Dixon smiled a little wearily. "You've sort of got the cart before the horse, Swayback," he replied. "I don't want to fight anybody; the Robertses are still fighting me."

"Guess that's putting it better," agreed Swayback. "Well, there's a way to stop it."

"How?" Dixon asked. Swayback countered with a question of his own.

"Read your history books, ain't you, son? Remember what stopped the Normans and the Saxons from fighting in England?"

"Why, what did?" Dixon asked.

"Well, it was this way," said Swayback. "They fought for a couple of hundred years after old Bill of Normandy came across the Channel and slapped the Saxons down. But the Norman fellers got to looking at the Saxon gals and marrying 'em. The Saxon fellers started doing the same with the Norman gals. So what happened? The Normans and the Saxons both found out that when they went and started a ruckus they were fighting the wife's relations, and when they came back from the shindig, there weren't no peace at home. Didn't take 'em long to get enough of *that*! So they settled down comfortably together, 'tendin' the farm and raisin' kids. Finally got to be what today we call the English folks."

Swayback paused, and his eyes twinkled at Dixon. "So," he resumed, "after you and Rosalee start pulling in double harness, I figure the fightin' between you and the Robertses will stop the same way."

Dixon smiled and shook his head. "Swayback," he said, "you're a nice old jigger, but I'm afraid you're a bit loco."

"Oh, no, I'm not," disclaimed Swayback. "I know the signs. I knew it that night when she came into the back room after you got bullet creased in that row down the street. She was madder'n a wet hen because somebody had done something to her man. Those big eyes of hers were just blazin', but when she turned 'em on you, they got all soft and cuddly. Can't fool old Swayback about that kind of a look in a gal's eyes. I'm glad of it. Rosy is a mighty nice gal and I want to see her get a good man, and if you hadn't come along when you did, she might have took Craig Sherwood."

"Took Craig Sherwood!" Dixon repeated.

"Uh-huh, women seem to take to that worthless wind spider, and I think he was sort of making headway with her before you showed up. And if she'd married him, she'd have been sorry. Rosy's a mighty pretty gal, but I've a mighty strong notion Sherwood was more interested in the Walking R than he was in her. He's the sort that'll do anything to get money for whisky and cards and other women. You see, Rosy owns half the Walking R."

"That's right," said Dixon. "She told me."

"Uh-huh, and you can bet Craig Sherwood ain't forgot. Wouldn't be surprised if Rosy knows he hasn't, too."

I've a notion she's still quite a bit interested in him," Dixon said gloomily. "Sure looked that way when they were together at this very table the last time I was up this way. She didn't even notice me when I came in."

Swayback's eyes twinkled again. "Son," he said, "you've got a lot to learn about women. What did you expect her to do—come running to you with her arms open? Remember, there's a bit of the kitty in the best of them. They sort of like to tease a man. And getting a man a mite jealous never hurt a girl's chances. Well, here comes your chuck; eat hearty."

Swayback knew exactly when to stop talking. With a nod and a grin he returned to the end of the bar, flinging a parting shot over his shoulder :

"Next time you run into her, drop a loop on her and haul her off to the sky pilot."

Dixon had to grin in return, although he was far from being as optimistic where Miss Roberts was concerned as Swayback appeared to be. He addressed himself to his food, but his mind was not on what he ate. In fact, if somebody had asked him whether he was surrounding steak or pork chops, he would have had difficulty answering.

Dixon and his hands headed for home the following morning. They laid over for the night at Muerto, and there they heard some news.

"The Robertses were in town," said John Cooley, the Silver Rail owner. "Said they ran into the wide-loopers again, just this side of the canyon. Seems Blount and the twins and Cliff White, their range boss, rode down there for a look-see. Said they were just starting to ford the river when the devils began throwing lead at them. Swore there was a couple hundred of the sidewinders. They turned tail and scooted for home. White got nicked in the shoulder; nothing serious, I reckon. The next night they rode down there with their whole outfit, and didn't see anything. Blount jumped the sheriff. Wanted to know why he didn't do something about it. Jarrett told him to get out or he'd lock him up for disturbing the peace. Blount got out."

Dixon and the others exchanged amused glances but kept their counsel.

"So it was the Robertses we saw hightailing away from there," Billy Flint remarked after Cooley had sauntered off. "Which sorta shows the bunch that tried to drygulch us wasn't the Robertses," he added thoughtfully.

" 'Fraid I'll have to agree with you," Bob Turner said grudgingly. "What the blazes *is* going on in this section?"

Dixon did not comment, but he was doing some hard thinking. So far as complicity in the abortive drygulching was concerned, it appeared the Robertses were exonerated. That is, he reflected gloomily, unless they had displayed an unusual ingenuity and had split up at the canyon mouth, four of their number riding northeast in plain sight to provide an excellent alibi and substantiate the story they took to town and the sheriff. He didn't really believe it was so; the Robertses just naturally weren't that smart.

On the other hand, it was ridiculous to think that an outlaw band to the south of the valley could have guessed what he and the sheriff had in mind and prepared against it. In the first place, wide-loopers didn't operate that way. They would have had nothing to gain and everything to lose by ambushing a sheriff's posse. Such an act would have aroused the whole section to an extent that would have made further raids on the valley out of the question.

Analysis of the incident permitted but two logical conclusions. Either his conviction with the sheriff had been overheard by the wrong pair of ears or Jarrett had carelessly let drop a seemingly innocuous remark that had been rightly interpreted.

By whom? If the Robertses were discarded, the only plausible suspect left, to Dixon's way of thinking, was Craig Sherwood. Dixon grimly resolved to get to the bottom of the whole mysterious business, if he managed to stay alive long enough.

Toying with his drink and absent-mindedly replying to the remarks of Flint and Turner, he gradually formulated a plan of action; a plan so fraught with danger that he determined not to enlist the aid of his companions and expose them to such hazards. He'd go it alone.

By so doing, if his deductions were sound, he knew he was pitting himself against a cold killer devoid of mercy or conscience who had an oufit of similar individuals at his back. Well, he'd gambled before, so why not one more throw of the dice against Fate, with death as the forfeit if he lost!

With the decision came a lightening of his spirits, and he joined with Flint and Turner in making the most of an evening in town.

CHAPTER FIFTEEN

AT AN EARLY hour the following morning, they headed for the Cross W. Flint and Turner were still chuckling over Nate Billings' panic and devising means to give him another scare at the first opportunity.

"Now if we can just get Blount Roberts where the hair's short, everything will be hunky-dory," declared old Bob.

They were approaching the point where the trail forked, the left branch—the old trail—veering slightly south eventually to pass the Cross W ranch-house, when they saw a girl sitting a big horse at the forks.

"By gosh, it's her!" exclaimed Billy Flint.

"Darned if it ain't!" agreed Turner.

Rosalee waved them a greeting as they drew near. Flint and Turner bobbed and grinned and quickened their pace as she reined in beside Dixon, leaving the pair to follow a little distance behind.

"Well, out with it," Rosalee said without preamble. "What happened the other night?"

"What do you mean?" Dixon evaded.

"I mean the row down by the canyon," she replied. "Blount and the twins and Cliff White, our range boss, were riding down that way when it cut loose. Blount said there hadn't been that much shooting since the Civil War. Said it was all up and down the valley. Was over by the trail at first; then got quiet. Then, just as

128

they were starting to ford the river, it cut loose again; only that time they were the targets. They went away from there in a hurry. Blount said if the light had been better the chances are some of them would have really gotten it instead of Cliff just getting a creased shoulder."

"Why were they riding down there?" Dixon asked.

"Because of something Cliff overheard in town," Rosalee replied.

Dixon's eyes narrowed a trifle. "What did he overhear?" he asked, trying to keep his voice casual.

"Craig Sherwood had ridden over for a visit and we were having a sociable gathering in the living-room when Cliff came in from town," Rosalee explained. "He said he was passing the sheriff's office and heard Floyd Jarrett say to you, 'I'll meet you down there tomorrow night.' Blount figured that 'down there' must mean the canyon, and he got so curious he decided to ride down to try and find out what was up. Guess later he wished he hadn't."

"And I suppose he blames me for what happened," Dixon remarked. Rosalee shook her red head. "Not exactly," she replied. "He believes you were mixed up in it somehow but can't figure just how. The fact that the sheriff was going to be along has him puzzled. He said that the first shooting they heard, over by the trail, sounded like two bunches had gotten together and were battling it out to a finish. He has to admit that your boys would hardly be shooting at each other. As to who threw lead at him, he can't say. So he had to be satisfied with saying everything was peaceful and quiet till you showed up in this section. Val, what did happen down there?"

Dixon told her, starting at the beginning, including

5—SRR

his own deductions and his interview with the sheriff. She listened intently, a pucker between her delicate brows.

"So it looks like there is a bunch raiding from the south," she commented when Dixon paused.

"It's pretty certain that there is a bunch raiding from somewhere," he replied grimly. There was no longer any doubt in his mind as to who that bunch was.

"A bunch raiding from somewhere," she repeated his words thoughtfully, and shot him a penetrating glance.

"And you don't think our boys have anything to do with it?" she asked.

"No," Dixon replied, "I don't. I think they've just been dupes, just as I have been."

Again the quick glance. "But you do think that a local outfit is back of it all?"

Dixon hesitated, at a loss how to answer. Finally he resorted to evasion and parried the question with one of his own:

"Does it seem reasonable that an outfit from the country to the south of the hills would have been able to deduce what the sheriff and I had in mind the other night?"

This time it was Rosalee who hesitated before replying. She gazed across the prairie for a long moment, giving him an excellent opportunity to realize how charming her profile was. Abruptly she turned to face him.

"No," she said. "No, it doesn't."

He watched fearfully for the next question, the question that would demand a positive answer. Val Dixon was still not at all sure that old Swayback Sawyer was right in his opinion as to just where Rosalee

Roberts' affections lay. He dreaded having to answer that question, but felt he could not lie to her or even evade. Sooner or later the truth was bound to come out; better to get it over with and let her face it. He drew a deep breath as once again she turned in the saddle; but when she spoke, what she said was utterly unexpected. She looked him steadily in the eyes, an her own were sorrowful.

"Val," she said, "I hate to say this, but I must. I have listened to what you have had to say, or rather, what was hidden beneath what you have said. It is a terrible thing to have one's faith in someone destroyed; someone for whom I once thought I might be able to care."

Dixon was startled and looked it. She smilingly shook her head.

"No, not you, my dear, if that's what's bothering you," she said. "My faith in you has never faltered since the day you spanked me for misbehaving, and what's more, it never will."

Dixon stared at her, scarcely daring to believe what her words seemed to imply. Suddenly she laughed, the gay, ringing laugh of a sublimely happy woman.

"Forgive me," she said, "but you look so scared, as if you were going to be married against your will. I hope it won't be against your will, because, my dear, you haven't a chance in the world to escape. The Robertses have a reputation for getting what they start out to get, and I'm no exception."

"Rosalee!" he faltered. "Do you really mean—"

"That's just exactly what I mean," she interrupted cheerfully. "I've been as thoroughly in love with you as you are with me from the first time we met, only you were too stupid to see it. It's most forward and unseemly for a girl to propose to a man, but I figured I'd have to or resign myself to being an old maid, and I don't think I'm old maid material.

"Oh, good gracious," she gasped, when she finally got a chance to use her lips for speaking. "You're shocking the horses! And what will the boys say if they happen to look back?"

"They'll say 'Hurrah!' " Dixon predicted happily. "They've made no bones about hoping this would happen."

Billy Flint did happen to glance back at that moment. He gazed at the pair riding so close together and chuckled.

"Bob," he said, "I've a notion our mavericking days are over. Bob, we've got a *home*!"

Rosalee's eyes suddenly became serious.

"Val," she said, "what are we going to do? The situation here is intolerable and appears to be getting no better fast."

Dixon bethought himself of old Swayback Sawyer's historical dissertation on the problems of the Normans and the Saxons and their final solution, but he recalled Swayback mentioning that it had taken a couple of hundred years to straighten things out via the marriage altar. He felt that was a bit too long to wait.

"I'm trying to work something out," he told her. "I believe it *will* work if I'm able to put the blame where it belongs, and prove it."

"If the boys can be shown that they have been made fools of by somebody, I think they can be persuaded to see reason," Rosalee said slowly. "For all his faults— and he's got plenty—Blount has something of his father's fairness and will acknowledge he is wrong when conclusively shown so. I think he is a bit bothered over the way he acted towards you. He honestly believed, in the beginning, that you were running off our cattle. Of course he was already prejudiced because you got the jump on him in the purchase of the Cross W from Samanthy Walsh, and was glad of any excuse to make trouble for you. I think you besting him in that knife fight gave him considerable of a jolt and, although you'd never get him to admit it, caused him to admire you secretly; he's made that way. Uncle Clanton has admitted that he probably made a mistake in riding over to your place and trying to tell you how to run your business. He'd been doing that with people for so many years I guess it was second nature for him where any newcomer was concerned."

"All of which at least gives us something to work on," Dixon summed up.

"That's the way I see it." Rosalee nodded.

"So it's up to me to prove to Blount and the others that they have been in the wrong," Dixon said. "Well, I'm going to try my best to do it."

"There'll be danger for you, won't there?" Rosalee asked.

"Oh, not particularly, if I'm careful," he returned lightly.

Plainly Rosalee didn't believe him. Her lips quivered a little and there were shadows in her expressive eyes.

"Really, I wish you wouldn't try it," she said.

"I must," he replied simply.

"Yes, I suppose you must," she conceded. "But please be careful—for my sake. I want a live husband, not a dead one."

"You may get both, for all you know," he teased.

"I'll be the judge of that," she answered.

When they reached the turn-off to the Cross W ranch-house, Rosalee drew rein.

"I'm going home," she said. "*Please* be careful, dear. I'll be waiting to hear how things turn out. That's a woman's cross—to wait!"

For a moment they clung together, indifferent to watching eyes. Then with a smile and a wave of her hand she rode away, and held back the tears until she was out of sight.

Supper in the big dining-room was a hilarious affair that night. Dixon tried to take part, but the problem in the back of his mind made it difficult to do so.

The following night, well after dark, Val rode east. He did not minimize the danger of the undertaking. If he were caught he could expect no mercy. And there was always the chance that he might ride into a nicely baited trap. Craig Sherwood had given ample evidence of his ability to anticipate an adversary's move and guard against it.

He continued to marvel at the paradox that was Sherwood's character. Despite the proof against him, Sherwood didn't seem to fit into the picture.

When Dixon reached the point where Sherwood's Forked S range began, he turned from the trail and rode across the shadowy prairie that was dimly lit by starlight and a cloudy half-moon. He still rode east, veering slightly to the south of the trail.

Finally he sighted the Forked S buildings, huddled together in a grove of very old live oaks. All around, the prairie was practically bare of growth, with only a few thickets at a short distance from the big and sprawling ranch-house that had been built by Craig Sherwood's grandfather.

From a distance, Dixon studied the ranch-house and its approaches. The result was not satisfactory. He noted a thicket only a few hundred yards from the *casa* that might afford concealment; but there was a long stretch of open ground he would have to cross to reach its dubious shelter. And he would be passing within easy rifle shot were someone on the watch. Not a pleasant prospect.

On the other hand, he felt it was unlikely that a guard would be posted in or near the building. Sherwood and his bunch would hardly expect anybody to come snooping around, unless the canny devil habitually was on guard against just such a possibility. Again unlikely, for it was logical to assume that Sherwood considered himself free from suspicion. At least Dixon hoped that would be his assumption. If not—

Oh, the devil with it! He'd set out to do a chore and he was going to do it no matter what the consequences. Drawing nearer he again paused to study his quarry. Now he was able to make out a door fronting south and towards what was undoubtedly the bunkhouse. It would be wise to avoid that door. He rode a wide circle a mile or so distant and approached from the east, keeping the thicket between him and the building. The gauze of cloud which had dimmed the stars and the moon had dissolved, and the night had turned brilliantly clear.

Dixon's pulses were pounding unpleasantly and the palms of his hands were moist as he drew nearer and nearer the dark and silent building beyond the thicket. He knew that any chance watcher could hardly miss spotting him. The mile he had to cover over the open ground seemed like a hundred. It was with a sigh of relief that he reached the sheltering growth and drew rein within its welcome sanctuary. He was breathing hard, as if he had done the juning instead of his horse.

Dismounting, he loosened the cinches, flipped the bit from the horse's mouth and turned it loose to graze on the tufts of dead-looking grass which grew between the mesquite trunks, which it seemed to think better than nothing. Wishing for the cigarette he dared not light, he took up his post at the edge of the growth, his gaze fixed on the dark buildings looming as soldier blocks of shadow in the pale moonshine.

Hour after hour he watched and listened. No sound broke the silence save the soft whispering of the wind in the branches over his head. Nothing moved within his range of vision; it was as if he alone were a living thing in a shadowy world of death. He hoped Rojo wouldn't take a notion to sing a song, for in the great stillness, the neigh of a horse would carry a long way and might well arouse suspicion. However, Rojo was usually a very silent horse, and he did not worry much on that score. But an occasional impatient stamp of a hoof sounded like a thunderclap and caused him to start, although it was highly improbable that the sound would carry to the ranch-house.

When the moon had set and the stars began to pale with the approach of dawn, he gave up. Too risky to wait until the light strengthened. It looked as if the Forked S denizens were sleeping the sleep of the just. Again he circled the site of the ranch-house and headed west at a fast pace, arriving at the Cross W before full daylight. He had learned nothing, but he was not discouraged; it was not likely he would get a break the first night of watching.

But as night after night he kept his tedious and lonely vigil with the same lack of results, he began to grow perturbed. Maybe he had been all wrong in his estimate of Sherwood. He and Rosalee had been in accord, although each had refrained from mentioning Sherwood's name. But Rosalee could also be wrong, subconsciously influenced, perhaps, by his own belief.

And then, the fifth night out, his doubts were resolved once for all, his judgement vindicated. Not long before midnight he approached the Forked S ranch-house with more than usual trepidation, for the almost full moon was shining brilliantly in a clear sky and the rangeland was nearly as bright as day. However, he reached the thicket without incident and made himself as comfortable as circumstances permitted. A couple of hours dragged past and the better part of a third. He disgustedly resigned himself to another night of fruitless watching. Then abruptly he stiffened, staring with intent eyes into the south-west.

Drifting over the prairie, silently as a company of ghosts, a band of horsemen approached at a rapid pace. Tense, eager, Dixon saw them draw near the ranch-house and turn into the yard. The cayuses were unsaddled and turned into the horse corral. The riders, several of them carrying saddle pouches, entered the ranch-house. Lights flashed on, sending yellow bars of radiance through the windows. Dixon's curiosity burned at a white heat. Where could the Forked S bunch have been riding in from the south-west at such an hour! He yearned for a look through one of the lighted windows. Intently he studied the building, noting that its rear lay in a deep shadow cast by the trees. Once in that shadow, he should have no difficulty slipping up to a window; but between him and the questionable refuge lay two hundred yards of moon-drenched prairie, across which a mouse couldn't pass without being seen by watching eyes.

But would there be any eyes watching the approaches to the building? Very likely the occupants of the house were occupied with various matters and not at all likely to be peering out of the windows. Should he risk it? He would be gambling with death if he did so; but for five nights he'd been waiting for just such an opportunity. He had hoped to see the Forked S outfit, Craig Sherwood at their head ride forth on some foray. His plan had been to follow them and see what they had in mind. Risky, yes; even more so than stealing up to the ranch-house under present circumstances. It looked very much as if they had *returned* from some questionable enterprise, probably having left the ranch-house at an early hour, before he arrived at the thicket.

"Horse," he said to Rojo, "here goes! I may come back in a hurry, so I'll get you all set to travel." With which he tightened the cinches, slipped the bit into place, knotted the split reins and draped them on the horse's neck. Then, after studying the lighted building for a moment, he stole from the thicket and, bending nearly double so as to provide as small a target as possible, scudded across the moon bright prairie. Every instant he expected to see flame gush from the shadows beneath the trees, followed by a report he very likely would not hear, a slug travelling somewhat faster than sound. He was gasping for breath when he straightened his aching back at the edge of the band of shadow. So far, so good!

For several minutes he leaned against a convenient tree until his heart stopped pounding; then he crept forward with the greatest caution, testing the ground with each step lest the sharp snap of a breaking dry stick or the click of a dislodged stone be heard inside the house. Often he paused to peer and listen. Reassured each time by the continued silence, broken only by a rumble of voices beyond the open window, he stole on until he reached the building wall. Then he inched along it to a point from which he could view the interior of what was evidently the living-room.

Over a table a hanging lamp burned, and around the tables were grouped nine men—Craig Sherwood and his force of riders.

But it was neither Sherwood nor the hard-faced cowhands that held Dixon's attention. The table was covered with money: stacks of gold pieces, packets of bills. Sherwood was writing figures on a sheet of paper.

"Eleven thousand and a couple of hundred over," he announced. "We've done better, but not bad! No, not bad."

A chuckle ran around the table as eyes gloated over the small fortune heaped on its top.

One man grumbled, however, a crooked-nosed individual who kept casting expectant glances at the closed outer door on the far side of the room.

"Why don't Walt hurry up with the whisky?" he demanded querulously. "Is he drinking it all himself?"

Hardly heeding this bit of byplay, Dixon strained his ears to catch what Craig Sherwood would say next— the words that would incriminate him and his men.

He never heard them. But he did hear a slight scuffling sound to his rear. He whirled to face a man who had crept up behind him; a man whose face was in the shadow, even as was his own. He caught the gleam of a knife flashing down in a vicious, plunging stroke.

CHAPTER SIXTEEN

IT WAS LUCKY for Val Dixon that he was an expert knife fighter. He had no blade of his own, but his left hand instinctively shot out in the natural parry for such a stroke. Wrist against the other's wrist, he deflected the steel, which ripped a gash in his forearm instead of driving straight in for his heart. In almost the same move he hit with his right. His fist smashed the fellow's mouth with all his weight behind it. The attacker gave a roar of pain, reeled back and fell. Dixon bounded over his prostrate form and tore through the grove. Inside the ranch-house sounded yells and curses and the clatter of overturned chairs.

A gun blazed behind him. The bullet came close. Another report and another slug, closer than the last. Then he was out of the grove and racing for the sanctuary of the thicket. The man he had hit continued to fire but he couldn't get the range. Then a whole volley cut loose. Slugs buzzed all around him. One slammed the heel of his boot and knocked him off balance. He went end over end like a plugged rabbit.

But the whoops of triumph changed to angry shouts as he scuttled forward on all fours, regained his feet and sped on. Only fifty yards to go! Maybe he could make it!

He did, diving into the growth, crashing through the underbush till he reached his snorting horse. He flung himself into the saddle, whirled Rojo and gave the golden horse his head.

His pursuers fired again when he came into view beyond the thicket, but now he was pretty well out of six-gun range, and evidently nobody had thought to fetch a rifle. Another moment and the firing ceased. Dixon rode on at top speed. He had no fear of pursuit, for he knew well Rojo could show a clean pair of heels to anything in the Forked S remuda, and before Sherwood and his men could saddle up, he'd have such a head start as to make overtaking him impossible. He did not believe he'd been recognized.

But what the devil was he to do? Ride to town and notify the sheriff? Notify him of what! That he had seen Sherwood and his men counting money? That one of Sherwood's hands had tried to knife him in the back?

"I'd be justified in getting the boys and riding up there and cleaning out the whole nest of snakes," he growled at Rojo. "Nope, that wouldn't do; I'd just get myself in trouble. Got to have more proof."

What next? He debated circling to the north and returning to the Cross W ranch-house, but decided not to. Just such a move might be anticipated, if by any chance he had been recognized, and he'd find himself surrounded. Better to go straight ahead to town; he wanted to consult with the sheriff, anyhow. He settled himself in the saddle and sent Rojo east along the trail.

Dawn was breaking when he arrived in Muerto, but the lights burned in the Silver Rail—the place never closed. Dropping the split reins to the ground beside a convenient hitchrack, he entered the saloon.

Only a sprinkling of die-hards were still at the bar

and the tables. John Cooley, the owner, was checking the day's receipts. Dixon approached him.

"Sheriff been around?" he asked casually.

Cooley shook his head. "Lit out for the Tornaga Trail, to the east and south of here, just before dark. Some masked hellions held up the stage that was packing payroll money to the Tornaga mines. Killed a guard and wounded the driver and got away with ten or fifteen thousand dollars. Jarrett was fit to be hogtied. Hard to tell when he'll be back. Said he figured to chase the snakes clean to Mexico if necessary."

Dixon whistled under his breath. So that was it! And he had watched Sherwood and his bunch counting the loot! He started to question Cooley further concerning the sheriff's movements when the saloon keeper interrupted him.

"Say!" he exclaimed, "your shirt sleeve's torn and there's blood on it. What you been into?"

"Steer was bogged in a mudhole and got me with his horn while I was hauling him out," Dixon explained glibly. "Just a scratch."

Cooley shot him a shrewd look but asked no further questions.

"Come on into the back room and I'll bandage it," he said. "I'm better'n Doc Beard at tying up bullet holes and—horn cuts. Guess you've heard before that a feller gets lots of practice in the likker business. Come along."

While Cooley worked on his gashed arm. Dixon again brought up the subject of the sheriff.

"Any notion when Jarrett will be back?" he asked.

"Hard to tell, but I'd say some time today will see him ride in cussin'. Those hellions are too much for poor old Floyd. A smart man heading that outfit of rapscallions, a mighty smart man."

With which Dixon was more than willing to agree. He thanked Cooley for his ministrations, had a drink with him and, after stabling his horse, secured a room for himself in the hotel and went to sleep. He didn't bother to awaken early. There was no hurry about his conference with Jarrett. Sherwood would have covered up long ago, and there would be no chance to pin the stage robbery on him. Better to let the sheriff get a little rest before taking up the matter. He'd be able to think better.

So he slept till noon, enjoyed a leisurely breakfast and a couple of cigarettes and then headed for the sheriff's office. He found the old peace officer in a very bad temper.

"Now what?" he demanded belligerently as Dixon entered and closed the door. "Supposing you're bringing me more trouble. All right, out with it! What have you been getting into?"

Dixon told him, in detail. As he listened, the sheriff's anger evaporated and was replaced by interest and amazement.

"Dixon," he said, "you sure you're not making this up or dreaming it?"

"Afraid not," Dixon replied. "What I'm telling you is the gospel truth."

"When did you first get suspicious of Sherwood?" the sheriff asked.

Starting at the beginning, Dixon outlined the series of happenings that had aroused his suspicions. The sheriff listened intently, tugging at his moustache and muttering from time to time, but otherwise not interrupting.

"The real payoff was when old Swayback Sawyer up in Lenton got to talking with me that night," Dixon concluded. "All of a sudden things began looking mighty clear."

"You make out a case against the hellion; and with Rosalee Roberts backing you up in it, I figure you're right all the way," said Jarrett. "She's a smart little tyke; always was. And a square-shooter like her dad.

"Funny," he added retrospectively, "things I didn't pay no mind to at the time are all of a sudden meaning something. When Sherwood came back here from Arizona or California, or wherever he was over west—he was always sorta vague about where he'd been—and took charge of the Forked S after his father died, he began having trouble with his hands, was always behind in their wages, until one by one they quit him. He hired others, fellers who came drifting along, chuck line riders and such. Gradually he got a bunch together that stuck with him. Now and then he'd hire some local hand, get behind with his pay, and the feller would quit, until he just had the bunch he'd picked up from here and there and everywhere. And as I said, those fellers stuck with him. Good cowhands, too, but not over sociable and not over well liked. Clannish sort of a bunch. And though he seemed to have trouble paying his hands, and always complaining that the ranch didn't pay off too well, he always had money for cards and likker and to spend on dance floor gals. Guess, like me, nobody ever gave it much thought, and Sherwood is the kind folks like. Always ready with a helping hand; always pleasant and sociable in spite of a hair-trigger temper that gets him in a row now and then. The Robertses think well of him and always have, and that goes for a lot in this section, or used to."

"He sure had me fooled," Dixon admitted. "I liked him, too, and I hate to think of him being mixed up in the things he is."

"Never can tell where the lightning will strike," the sheriff observed sententiously. "I've seen fellers you'd never suspect go bad. Yes, that was the Tornaga mines payroll money you saw them counting. No doubt as to that. Well, anyhow, now we know who to look for when something else is pulled."

"Hope I didn't scare him into hunting cover for good," Dixon remarked.

"Not likely," said the sheriff. "Unless they recognized you, the chances are they figured it to be just some chuck line-riding cowpoke prowling around. Take more than that to stop them. Sherwood has to keep on working to keep his hellions supplied with money; that sort gets rid of it fast. Plenty of places besides Muerto where they can do their drinking; they never show up in Muerto much. We'll just lay low till something busts loose; then we'll land on them like forty hen hawks on a settin' quail."

But as the days passed and grew into weeks, Dixon began to wonder if the sheriff could be wrong. He had work to occupy him, however; preparations had to be made for the coming winter, and everybody was busy from dawn till nightfall. Twice Rosalee rode to the Cross W ranch-house.

"After swearing him to secrecy, I told Uncle Clanton we were going to get married, and darned if he didn't approve!" she announced to the surprised Dixon. "He said you appeared to be a steady young man and should make good at anything you set your hand to. Nice of him, don't you think?"

"Very nice, and most unexpected," Dixon replied. "Now if you can just get the rest of the family to feel the same way."

"It's not going to be easy," she admitted. "Blount is stubborn and vindictive, and the twins will follow his lead."

Abruptly the points of light that Dixon loved to see were in her eyes. Her red lips tightened.

"If it didn't mean kicking up a holy row that might end in real trouble, I'd tell them all and make them take it," she declared. "A little more and I *will* kick over the traces."

"Right now suits me," Dixon said.

She smiled a little tremulously. "Be patient just a little longer, dear," she pleaded "I'll admit that if you insist, I won't say no to you, but I hope you'll agree to wait just a little while; maybe we'll get a break. What you told me about what you saw at the Forked S ranch-house makes it look like we will."

Dixon reluctantly agreed.

More uneventful days passed. And then one evening just before dusk, Sheriff Jarrett rode into the ranch-house yard.

"Looks like this is it," he told Dixon. "They're branching out. Hit the railroad again early this morning; this time way over to the west and north. Wrecked the Alpine local and grabbed a money transfer to the Alpine bank. Got better than thirty thousand dollars, their biggest haul to date. Not in my bailiwick this time; happened just the other side of the country line. But of course I was notified and told to keep a look-out for them over this way. They'll have a long ride to get back to their hangout by way of trails nobody but their sort knows. I figure they'll make it in around daylight tomorrow, and we'll be ready for them. Oh, it was Sherwood and his bunch, all right. All masked, of course, but used methods similar to those employed in other jobs. Yep, I'll have a cup of coffee and a snack; we're in no hurry. Then call your boys in and give them the lowdown. I'll deputize them as a posse and we'll be all set. I don't think there'll by any slip-ups this time. I rode west out of the town, circled around the other side of the river and hit the trail down this way. Kept a careful watch to make sure I wasn't wearing a tail and didn't spot anybody trailing me. This time we'll get 'em."

Most of the Cross W boys expressed astonishment when told what was in the wind, but Billy Flint only shrugged.

"Told you the first time I saw him that I didn't like that hellion," he remarked to Dixon. "Don't surprise me a bit to learn he rides the owlhoot trail. I would have said so a while back, only I figured everybody would say I was loco. I've known too many of his sort to be fooled by the kind of front he puts on."

"Uh-huh, wouldn't be surprised if you've known quite a few of that sort," the sheriff observed dryly.

Billy grinned his twisted grin and twinkled his cold eyes at him. "You should have been around when I headed a *bandido* bunch down in *mañana* land," he chuckled.

"I'm darned glad I wasn't," the sheriff declared heartily amid a general laugh.

It was long past midnight when Sheriff Jarrett and his

posse rode east. They reached the thicket where Val Dixon had passed so many weary nights, dismounted and tethered their horses. Below them the Forked S ranch-house lay dark and silent, with no sign of occupancy. The brilliant moonlight showed the horse corral to be almost empty. Jarrett proceeded to outline his plan of campaign.

"We might as well take it easy for a spell," he said; "they'll never make it in till past sun-up. When it begins to get light, one man will stay here to mind the horses and keep them quiet whilst the rest of us slide down there and take up positions behind the trees. They'll be riding in from the south-west and won't spot us if we're careful and keep under cover. Let them unfork before we make a move; otherwise some of them may give us the slip. When I give the word, slide out and cover them. Chances are they won't give up without a fight, but the advantage should be on our side. If it does come to a fight, shoot straight and shoot fast. You're up against a nest of sidewinders from whom you can't expect any mercy if they get the upper hand. Okay, everybody understand?"

There was a general nodding of heads.

The wait that followed was long and tedious. Even more tedious was the wait behind the trees that surrounded the ranch-house. The sun rose, glinting on the leaves. Birds sang cheerfully. Cattle bleated in the distance. The possemen stood motionless behind their trees. Dixon's nerves were tightening like piano wire, his palms sweating. He strained his eyes across the brightening prairie, hoping to see the approaching horsemen. Anything would be better than this intolerable waiting.

The sun rose higher, flooding the rangeland with golden light. Dixon relaxed a little and glanced at Billy Flint concealed behind the next tree. Abruptly the cowboy spoke.

"Here they come!"

Dixon's head jerked around. Far to the south-west was a clump of little bouncing dots. As he watched they swiftly grew in size, were identifiable as horsemen approaching at a fast pace.

"Get set," said the sheriff.

Up to the ranch-house swept the hard-riding troop, Craig Sherwood in the lead; saddle pouches were plumped out. Pulling to a jingling halt, the Forked S riders dismounted, grouping together and unbuckling the stuffed pouches. Sheriff Jarrett's voice rang out,

"In the name of the State of Texas, you are under arrest. Get your hands up! You're covered!"

The grouped riders whirled to stare into the drawn guns of the posse. Hands began to rise. Craig Sherwood stood rigid, his eyes blazing with maniacal fury.

"Blast you, Dixon!" he screamed, and went for his gun. The two reports blended almost as one. Dixon stood firm and erect, but Sherwood reeled back and fell, to lie motionless, arms widespread. His followers were all drawing and shooting. The posse's answering volley was a drumroll of horrific sound.

Ralph Boyd yelled a curse as a slug smashed his shoulder. Sheriff Jarrett was down, shot through the leg. Jim Carstairs was reeling about, his face streaming blood, dazed by a bullet that had grazed his skull.

In seconds it was all over. Five of the outlaws were on the ground beside their leader. Three others had their hands in the air, yelling for mercy.

"Hold it!" Dixon shouted to his men. "Grab them and tie them up. Are you hurt much, Jarrett?"

The sheriff replied with a flood of profanity. "I'm all right," he concluded. "Scared I can't walk, though. See if Sherwood is dead."

Dixon moved to do so, while his hands disarmed the cringing outlaws. Nobody had noticed approaching from the east a rider who had jerked his mount to a halt as the shooting started, stared a moment, then had whirled and fled to the concealment of a thicket a mile away.

Sherwood was still alive but going fast. He gazed up at Dixon, who knelt beside him, and the ghost of a smile touched his pallid lips.

"End of the trail, Dixon," he whispered. "End of a crooked trail. I knew you meant trouble for me when you showed up in this section. Knew you couldn't be buffaloed by the Robertses or anybody else. Tried to have you done away with a few times. Tried to have you robbed in Lenton. Had your barn burned, figuring you'd blame the Robertses. Kept on trying to stir up trouble between you and the Robertses, hoping they'd do for you and maybe you'd do for them. May happen yet, but it won't do me any good. Figured after I got control of the Walking R I'd settle down and go straight. Can't straighten—a—crooked—trail!" His eyes closed as if in sleep and he was dead.

While the wounded were being cared for, Dixon paused beside the body of a big, thick-shouldered man who had been shot through the head.

"Don't recall seeing this one before," he remarked.

"That's Ad Travis," said one of the prisoners, a scrawny little runt with shifty eyes who appeared ready to talk. "Him and Jess Willoughby used to get the lowdown on the jobs we pulled. They were mighty good at that. You remember Jess, don't you? You killed him in Lenton."

Dixon nodded without speaking. That was when he had started being a killer, and he didn't like being reminded of it.

The sheriff was carried into the ranch-house and made as comfortable as possible; the other wounds, which were not serious, had been treated.

"Now what?" Dixon asked.

"Scared I can't ride just yet," Jarrett replied, "so you'd better take the prisoners to town and turn them over to Deputy Hawkins; he'll be at the office. Might as well pack along the money that's in those pouches, and the carcases. Tell Hawkins everything that happened. See if you can rustle some coffee and a bite to eat before you go; I can stand both. Darn this leg, anyhow!"

CHAPTER SEVENTEEN

MOST OF THE Walking R hands were busy at chores around the corrals, the blacksmith shop and other buildings, Blount Roberts superintending, old Clanton pottering about, when a wild-eyed cowboy rode a foaming horse into the yard.

"Dixon and his bunch raided Sherwood's place and killed everybody," he shouted. "I was just riding up when the shooting started. I hightailed, holed up in the brush and watched. Was too far away to see everything, but I did see Dixon and his hellions head for Muerto."

Blount Roberts, his face crimson with anger, swore an explosive oath. "That blasted range tramp is out to do us all in," he raged. "It's showdown! All right, he asked for it. We're heading for town to have it out with him once and for all."

"Hold it, Blount," cautioned old Clanton. "Wait till you get the straight of things before you go off half-cocked."

"I've got them straight enough," Blount replied viciously. "Come on, boys!"

Old Clanton, his eyes dark with foreboding, watched them thunder out of the yard. He turned and lumbered to the ranch-house and met Rosalee coming down the stairs.

"What in the world has happened?" she asked.

Clanton told her. Without a word she sped to the stable where her pet saddle horse was stalled.

Progress was slow because of the bodies roped to the backs of the horses, and it was well past noon when the posse reached town. Muerto seethed with excitement as the grim cavalcade passed down the main street to the sheriff's office. A crowd followed and peered in the door and windows as Dixon explained what had happened.

With many profane ejaculations, Deputy Hawkins locked up the prisoners, laid out the bodies on the floor and stowed the stolen money in the safe.

"And I guess that's all," Dixon concluded wearily. "You'd better take a buckboard down to the ranch-house tomorrow morning to fetch the sheriff back. He's resting easy but is in no shape to ride. I left Bob Turner and a couple of my hands to look after him. Come on, boys. Let's go get a drink; I feel in the need of one."

As they walked up the street they saw a group of riders dismounting in front of the Silver Rail. Billy Flint uttered an exclamation.

"It's the Robertses," he said. "Val, there's going to be trouble. Blount Roberts looks like a crazy man."

"I hope not," Dixon replied, "but if there is, try not to kill anybody; try to disarm or cripple. Scatter out, you fellows; don't bunch together."

Blount Roberts was striding forward, his face convulsed. "You murderer!" he yelled.

Dixon stared at him in amazement. "What's the matter with you Roberts, have you gone loco?" he called back. "Hold up till I explain."

Nobody seemed to know for sure just how it started, but it was generally agreed that somebody pulled a gun, and the ball was open! The street fairly exploded to the roar of six-shooters.

But, contrary to popular opinion, cowhands are usually poor shots, and the distance was considerable. Dixon was trying to disarm Blount Roberts; Billy Flint was shooting at arms and legs. Men fell on both sides, cursing, or staggered away with yelps of pain. Dixon lined sights with Blount's gun hand and heard the hammer of his Colt click on an empty shell. Blount leaped forward with a yell of triumph and took deliberate aim at Dixon's breast just as a girl on a lathered horse dashed up and swung from the saddle with her mount still going at full speed.

"No, Blount! No!" she screamed, and darted in front of Dixon. Blount's gun spurted fire and, with a gasping moan, Rosalee fell in a pathetic little heap at Dixon's feet.

The shooting stopped. Men stood aghast. Blount Roberts, his eyes wild with horror, reeled as if struck by a mighty fist; the gun dropped from his nerveless hand.

From the veranda of Doc Beard's office came a stentorian roar:

"Bring her in here, Dixon! Bring her in here! You loco hotheads, I hope you're satisfied!"

As Dixon gathered Rosalee's limp form in his arms, Doc Beard stormed down the steps to face Blount Roberts.

"And as for you, I hope you never sleep again! I hope you see her dead face every hour of the day! I hope you burn through all eternity, you stinkin' cross between a rattlesnake and a hydrophobia skunk!"

Blount shrank back from the white wrath of the old man. He cowered before him like a dog before some savage master, armed with a whip. Doc whirled and raced up the steps after Dixon, Billy Flint following close behind. Doc shouted over his shoulder, "Cooley, tie up those punctured hellions or leave 'em to bleed to death, I don't care which; I haven't time to fool with them.

"The inner room," he told Dixon. "Put her on the table there. And then get out, both of you, and shut the door; I'll call you if I want you. Yes, she's still alive, but that's about all. Get out!"

When the door was closed, Doc instantly set to work, baring the wound, a small blue hole beneath the left breast, from which a blood bubble rose and fell.

"Wind wound!" he muttered. "Bad!"

Gently he explored the girl's back with sensitive fingers, and found no corresponding opening. He snatched his stethoscope, placed it against her chest and listened intently for some moments. The lines in his face seemed deeper as he laid the instrument aside and began pacing the floor, muttering to himself:

"If I don't operate she's a goner, and how can I perform such an operation without an experienced anaesthetist and trained help!"

He glanced at the girl again and shook his head. She was breathing in little gasps, and at each breath the blood bubble frothed. Doc turned to the door, opened it and entered the outer room. Dixon and Flint gazed at him with fearful expectancy.

"She's in bad shape," Doc said without preamble.

"The thing's inside her chest. It's pressing against the aorta, the great trunk artery which carries blood from the heart to be distributed by branch arteries through the body. As the heart beats, the artery pulses and swells. The slug chafes against it. Only a matter of time till it wears through the wall of the aorta, which will result in a massive hemorrhage and death. That slug must be removed if she is to live, but if I attempt such an operation by myself without proper assistance, the chances are I'll kill her. That's how the situation stands. If nothing's done, it's only a matter of hours, and not too many hours at that. I'm going back there to think and try and figure something. Don't let anybody in."

He returned to the inner room and the almost lifeless form on the operating table, and closed the door.

In the outer room, Dixon sat white and numb, his sweating hands opening and closing, his lips twitching. There was a horrible crawling sickness in the pit of his stomach, a dull roaring in his head. His unseeing eyes were fixed stonily on the closed door. For once in his life Val Dixon knew the meaning of stark terror, the agony of utter helplessness. All his strength was nothing. The drive which had propelled him to material success was as mist upon the face of the water. She was about to be taken from him, and in the darkness of his storm-tossed soul thundered a realization of the true values; all else was but vanity.

A slight sound on the far side of the room attracted his attention. Billy Flint, the man of steel, the cold killer, was kneeling beside the closed door, his hands clasped in front of him, his head bent.

Dixon gazed and gazed, and suddenly a great peace flooded over him.

"God," he murmured, "if You can bring Billy Flint to his knees, You can pull her through! I know You can, and You will! I'm not scared any more."

He got up softly and went out into the sunlight.

The street was strangely silent. The wounded had been led or carried into the Silver Rail, where John Cooley ministered to their hurts. Men stood about in hushed groups.

In the middle of the road was a single figure, tortured eyes fixed on the doctor's office. Blount Roberts' back was bowed, his shoulders hunched; he looked like an old, old man. He shambled forward a few steps, his eyes pleading, as Dixon appeared.

"Dixon," he said hoarsely, "I didn't mean to do it. As God is my witness, I didn't mean to do it!"

"I know you didn't, Blount," Dixon said gently.

In Blount's eyes was born something akin to hope.

"I didn't mean to do it," he repeated, "but I did, and I'm all to blame. I was wrong from the beginning, wrong in everything I did to you. Dixon, could we forget it all and start over?"

"I don't see any reason we can't," Dixon replied.

Blount stared at him a moment. "Maybe we could be friends," he said haltingly.

"Why not?" Dixon asked.

Blount straightened a little. Hesitantly he thrust out his hand. "You'll take my hand on it?"

Dixon's answer was to hold out his own. Looking into each other's eyes, the two big men gripped hands in a clasp of friendship.

"How is she?" Blount asked.

"Pretty bad," Dixon replied. "Doc says if he doesn't

operate, it's only a matter of time, and he's afraid to operate without proper assistants."

Blount Roberts suddenly straightened his back and squared his shoulders.

"Come on," he said; "we're heading for the telegraph office. I know a man in San Antonio, a surgeon, the best in the world at this sort of thing. He's Dad's friend. I'll get him. I know the General Division Superintendent of the railroad. He'll give up a special train to get him here. Come on!"

Blount Roberts was as good as his word. Within the hour a special train was roaring westward to Lenton, where the fastest horses available waited.

In an incredibly short time the surgeon arrived. He shook hands with Blount and was introduced to Billy Flint and Val Dixon, at whom he gazed with eyes of compassion. The doctor was used to sorrow, but this man's suffering unnerved him; he turned from it and entered the inner room.

An hour passed, an hour of torture for the three who sat silent in the doctor's office, and the better part of a second.

At last the eternity ended. The door opened and the surgeon appeared. His face was tired and lined, but he was smiling.

"She'll make it," he said. "It was touch and go for a while, but the operation was a complete success. She's small but sturdy. I doubt if she ever had a sick day in her life. She could be up and about in a week, and her normal self in a couple more. I'm going across the street for a drink; my assistants will take care of tidying up."

He gazed at the three men standing shoulder to shoulder, unutterable relief in their eyes, and listened to their broken words of thanks. With a smile and a nod he left the room.

The doctor was right in his prediction. Rosalee's recovery was rapid. Within a week she was on her feet, and Val Dixon did not leave town till she was up and about.

Among other unusual things for a frontier town, Muerto boasted a church. It was not a very big church, and one afternoon, a month after the fight in front of the Silver Rail, it was crowded to overflowing. The Cross W and the Walking R outfits sat together in good fellowship, beaming proudly. Billy Flint was best man, and a dance floor girl from the Silver Rail was maid of honour.

As he opened his book at a certain page, the old clergyman, who had spent a lifetime in service to the frontier people, smiled with quiet contentment as he gazed at the symbol of the peace that at long last had come to Star Drive Valley.

Outside the church, Val Dixon looked down at his pretty little wife. She crinkled her eyes at him.

"And now what do you want?" he asked uneasily, for there was never any telling what turn her impish sense of humour would take. Rosalee giggled.

"I think," she said, "I wouldn't mind another spanking!"

Leslie Scott was born in Lewisburg, West Virginia. During the Great War, he joined the French Foreign Legion and spent four years in the trenches. In the 1920s he worked as a mining engineer and bridge builder in the western American states and in China before settling in New York. A barroom discussion in 1934 with Leo Margulies, who was managing editor for Standard Magazines, prompted Scott to try writing fiction. He went on to create two of the most notable series characters in Western pulp magazines. In 1936, when Standard Magazines launched *Texas Rangers*, Scott under the house name of Jackson Cole, created Jim Hatfield, Texas Ranger, a character whose popularity was so great with readers that this magazine featuring his adventures lasted until 1958. When others eventually began contributing Jim Hatfield stories, Scott created another Texas Ranger hero, Walt Slade, better known as *El Halcon*, the Hawk, whose exploits were regularly featured in *Thrilling Western*. In the 1950s Scott moved quickly into writing book-length adventures about both Jim Hatfield and Walt Slade in long series of original paperback Westerns. At the same time, however, Scott was also doing some of his best work in hardcover Westerns published by Arcadia House, thoughtful, well-constructed stories, with engaging characters and authentic settings and situations. Among the best of these, surely, are *Silver City* (1953), *Longhorn Empire* (1954), *The Trail Builders* (1956) and *Blood on the Rio Grande* (1959). In these hardcover Westerns, many of which have never been reprinted, Scott proved himself highly capable of writing traditional Western stories with characters who have sufficient depth to change in the course of the narrative and with a degree of authenticity and historical accuracy absent from many of his series stories.